falling

DANSBORO CROSSING
BOOK 5

AVERY SAMSON

Editor: My Brother's Editor

Cover Designer: Rachel Webb

Cover Photo: Jane Ashley Photography

contents

one

PETER

"COME ON, G. You know you want to do it." I've been whining at Geneva since we made it back from Texas. I think it's starting to work. We only have a day before we leave if she's going to agree.

"Why would I want to be stuck in your car driving cross-country when I can sit in first class and be there in a few hours?"

I bet you thought I'd been trying to convince her to have sex with me. Get your mind out of the gutter. Although I'm definitely on board with that idea, but, no. I've been trying to convince her to road trip with me from sunny San Francisco to even more sunny Austin.

We both took a leap of faith when we resigned from her father's real estate development business to join her brother in Texas. He fell in love with a one-night stand and never returned to California.

I wholeheartedly approve of the choice he made. He's

now married with a beautiful baby boy to fuss over. We agreed quickly that a struggling new business in Texas was better than dealing with her abusive father, even if it was lucrative.

I've been friends with Rand since boarding school. We were thrown together in middle school as roommates. The first time I met his sister, Geneva, she was tall, thin, and had a look that could freeze water.

Not much has changed. Except now, I really like when her icy gaze is turned on me. But she's my best friend's sister. She's off limits, but that doesn't mean she's not always on my mind.

"Think about it. We could stop by Yosemite and Zion. You know you've always wanted to ride the rims." It's a wild guess. Honestly, I don't know that much about either park. I don't know a thing about riding a horse either, but whatever. It's just been a long time since I've done anything other than work. I want an adventure. And I don't want to go alone.

"I do like horses," she admits.

"There you go."

"And rims." She smiles wickedly. Don't read anything into it. We've been doing this barely civil sexual innuendo thing for years. I think we started it in an effort to freak her brother the fuck out. It worked, so we kept doing it. Now, I wonder if we even notice what we say to each other anymore.

"We could raft the Grand Canyon," I dangle.

Her eyes narrow at me. That means that she's either seriously considering going or I'm going to wake up in the hospital in several days. Did I mention the woman has a black belt in some sort of martial arts? She can probably raft like a demon too. I might be getting in over my head.

"Fine," she says.

She's sitting on my couch among the boxes waiting to be moved to Austin tomorrow. Her long legs stretch to the coffee table, where she wiggles her toes. Luscious, suckable toes. Jesus. I need to get laid. Not that Geneva's not all kinds of hot, but she's still my best friend's sister. Although I get a kick out of telling him she's hot all the time.

"Stop staring at my feet, perv."

"Yes or no, Geneva."

"Fine."

Something inside me is doing a little cheer over spending a week on the road with this sex goddess. Probably the cheerleaders of Boner U.

"But we're hiking in Yosemite, riding in Zion, and rafting the Grand Canyon."

I'm going to die.

"And..."

I wait for more demands.

"Shopping in Santa Fe."

"Seriously?" I ask. I'm not that worried about being dragged around the shops in Santa Fe. I doubt I'll still be alive at that point.

"Yes, seriously. I want to check out the art galleries."

"Fine." Who cares? I really will already be dead.

"Fine." She glares at me, seeing if she can call my bluff. I've known Geneva since her family came to deliver her brother to boarding school. She was eleven at the time and just as obstinate. Her mother fussed over Rand's side of the room while Geneva stared at me with the same glare she's giving me now.

"Yes, fine. I'll pack my glasses so I don't get a headache." I'm color blind. It's never hindered my ability to design buildings or render plans. I just always check with her to make sure my color elevations are correct.

Art galleries, however, are a dizzying riot of chaos to my eyes. I have both color-correcting glasses and sunglasses.

"I guess I should go home and finish packing," she says with a sigh.

"Would you like dinner first?" Food is most likely the reason she's in my apartment in the first place. I've never seen Geneva so much as boil water. I, however, took all the culinary classes they'd let me take while at college. I like to cook, and I wanted to do it well.

"What are you making?"

"French toast."

"Your cinnamon swirl french toast?"

"The one and only."

She closes her eyes on a moan. Damn. I wish I could get her to make that sound by doing something other than talking about food.

"You're such a tease." She grins. "Fucking sadistic."

I laugh and get the only mixing bowl not in a box out of the cabinet. The cinnamon bread I made last night, so I know it's fresh. My remaining eggs get cracked into the bowl. I add a touch of cinnamon, vanilla, and milk. Geneva moves to the bar to watch me work. This is one of her favorites, which is why I saved the ingredients for tonight.

The move to Austin seems to be harder on Geneva than on Rand or me. She left a job she was confident in, a Jiu-Jitsu instructor she liked, and a modern-designed apartment she adored.

I know she'll shine at the new company we're forming. But I wonder if she knows that. Geneva is as tough as they come on the outside. But on the inside, I think there's more than meets the eye.

"How is it?" I ask, watching her take the first bite of french toast. She closes her eyes and chews for several minutes. Her eyes pop back open, spearing me with that cerulean gaze. It's something she does all the time; she knocks me on my ass with that look. It steals my breath away every damn time.

"Panty melting," she purrs.

"Then my job here is done." She smiles and takes another bite. "The movers are supposed to be here around seven tomorrow morning. It shouldn't take them long, then we'll head to your place. I have everything we should need on our trip, so just pack any personal items you want to take."

"Do I need anything specific?" she asks with a wink. She is the adventure seeker, not me. I visualize a pack worthy of someone preparing to climb Everest.

"Make sure you pack layers. We'll leave as soon as the truck pulls out."

"I guess I should go then. Just finding the box my hiking boots are in should prove a challenge. Thanks for dinner." She stands and moves to the door. "Peter?"

"Yeah." I wait for what she's going to say. She seems to be on the brink of saying more but then reconsiders.

"See you tomorrow."

Then she's gone. I wish she had just said what she wanted to. Ever since I've known her, she's had a wall firmly in place. Not just on my account either. No one that I've ever seen gets all of her.

I've never challenged her on that wall. I understand why it's there. It took me a year of living in a dorm room with Rand to earn his trust enough to learn that the house they grew up in was one of violence. The best thing their mother did was send them to boarding school. Unfortunately, it was on opposite sides of the country.

The only support Geneva had in her young life was ripped away from her when Rand left for New England. She was left with an angry father, a barely existent mother, and a rebellious streak a mile long.

But sometimes the devil you know is better than the unknown. When Rand went to work for his father, he brought me with him. Geneva joined us the next year, and I got a first-hand look at the control Joseph Randolph had over his children.

Now, they've found their way out. Rand is living happily with his wife and new baby, the result of the best accident to ever happen to him. And Geneva is moving to a new city to join us in forming a new company.

I think this trip will be as important for her in making the transition as it is to me. I just hope we can survive a week of hiking, riding, rafting, and each other.

* * *

The movers show up bright and early the next morning. I've decided to donate or sell most of my stuff. Nothing like embracing the idea of starting life over with new things. As a result, it doesn't take long to load out what's left. A couple of hours later, I pull up outside Geneva's apartment.

"Hey," I say when she meets me. She seems a little skittish today. "Are you okay?"

"I'm good. Can we just get this done?" she snaps. I nod and lead the movers upstairs. Geneva has a lot more she's moving than I do. It takes several more hours for everything to be loaded into the truck.

We're close to being done when I notice her standing in

the corner of her living room, wringing her hands. I slide next to her and drape an arm over her shoulder. I squeeze her against my side.

A shuddering breath escapes her lips. My arms wrap around her as I pull her against my chest. For a couple of seconds, she lets me comfort her. Then she shoves me away. I'm not offended; that's just Geneva.

"Let's blow this place," she says, her jaw set in determination. We lock up and turn the keys into the concierge. Cleaners come tomorrow to clean both of our places.

Unlike Rand, neither of us owns our place. I had to pay a penalty for moving out early. Geneva only had two months left on her lease. There was a list of new tenants waiting for her place, so they waived any fees.

"Let me give you the grand tour of our steed for the next week." I unlock my Land Rover. It's not new, but it gets me where I need to go. Right now, it's full of everything I think we might need for a road trip.

"This is the easy-to-reach cooler full of both water and soda. Don't lecture me about sugar," I add, holding up my hand when Geneva cocks a hip. "This one is snacks, both healthy and junk."

"Nuts?"

"Lightly salted and chocolate covered. Also, chips, rice cakes, granola, cheese, the list goes on." She peers in the back, looking skeptical. "Just get in." She rolls her eyes but climbs in the passenger seat. I take a couple of deep breaths and walk to the driver's side.

"Are we there yet?" she asks when I slide in.

"There are a couple of game books in the door to keep you entertained the whole three and a half hours to Yosemite." She rolls her eyes and pulls out her phone. "Hey, no phones. You have to keep me awake."

She puts her phone down. Digging through the stash of game books and magazines I picked up yesterday, she pulls one out. "Ooh, a survey."

Crap. I should have chosen better.

"Tell us about your first time."

What you're about to witness is Geneva's ability to torture me to the point of madness. She's been perfecting it since we were young. There are probably a dozen articles we could discuss, but she's zeroed in on the one that will push me the farthest out of my comfort zone. Well, I guess when in Rome...

"Fire away." I chance a glance at her. Her eyes gleam back at me.

"Question one. How would you best describe the experience? One, it was a special and exciting experience. Two, it was uncomfortable at times but still good. Three, it was awkward and I'm glad I got it over with. Or four, it was a disaster."

"Umm." I have to think about this one for a minute. "I guess it was somewhere between exciting and awkward. She was older. She was way more experienced than I was. I fumbled around until she finally lost patience and took over."

"Alright. Question two."

"No, no. That's not how we're playing this. Now, it's your turn to answer." She tries to wait me out, but we have three more hours to go. I can hold out forever.

"Fine," she finally growls. "It was time to get past being a virgin. I picked up a guy. We had sex. It was neither good nor bad; it just was."

That's horrible. I would take nervous fumbling over that any day. My heart breaks thinking this is what she chose. I've heard her be called a cold fish and worse before. It's not true, though. I think she just uses it as a defense.

"Question two," she starts again. "Were you nervous?"

"Hell, yes."

"What about? That's question three, by the way."

"About everything. Am I doing something wrong? Is the condom still good? What if she doesn't want to see me again? I know you think I'm this super stud, but I'm really a very insecure person inside."

I laugh. She doesn't.

"You're probably the most secure person I've ever met. You've always had your shit together, Peter. Not like Rand and I. Well, Rand is getting there."

She couldn't have shocked me any harder if she had hooked me up to the car battery and poured water on my head. I've always felt like she thought I was a moron.

"What about you?" I ask.

"Didn't think about it." She smirks this time. I don't think it's far from the truth. "He was pretty drunk anyway, so I had to do most of the work."

"Were you nervous?"

"Why? I planned it. I told you, it was just sex."

"It should never be just sex," I argue.

"Question four," she continues, cutting me off. "Were you aroused?" She wiggles her eyebrows, making me chuckle.

"Obviously enough."

"Yeah, he was totally into it. Even if he was slurring his words." She doesn't mention if she was, and I don't want to hear the same answer again. "What position did you use?"

"Missionary," we announce at the same time.

"Jinx, you owe me a soda," she adds. I point to the back

seat. She digs her favorite diet out of the cooler. She pops it open and turns back to the magazine.

"How old were you?"

"Seventeen," I answer. "She was nineteen. Your brother and I snuck out of the dorms to attend a college party. We hitchhiked to the train station. Still made it back before morning call." I wait for her to answer the same question. I hope I don't hate the answer.

two

GENEVA

PETER WINSLOE IS without a doubt the most honorable person I've ever known. Hell, he's probably the most honorable person anyone who's ever met him knows.

I know that sounds old-fashioned, which is sad, really. This world could use more men like him. Rand and I agree that Peter is the best of us. I'm sure he has flaws; I know he does. They're just hard to see around the shining armor.

He was raised by parents who, while lacking money, provided all the love and support a child would need. Hugs and "good jobs" were handed out in equal supply between him and his four siblings. His parents still hold hands after thirty years of marriage. They call him every Thursday night just to tell him they love him. They're those people.

That's how I know he's going to hate my answer. "Fourteen."

"Fourteen?" He says it like he's casting a curse. "Fourteen?" As if saying it louder changes the answer. "Geneva, what were you thinking? Fourteen is way too young. Hell, seventeen was too young."

"Okay, Dad."

"It's not funny." He runs a hand down his face. Peter has a lot of tells when it comes to emotions. This particular one means he's frustrated. I've studied him for years now. I know every non-verbal cue he has. "Jesus. Why didn't Rand tell me?" he mumbles to himself.

"Rand doesn't know," I snap. "Rand doesn't need to know. Rand isn't going to know."

It's not an idle threat, and Peter knows it. Rand would completely lose his shit about it. I shouldn't have told Peter. He's like having another, much hotter brother. The brother I'd like to see naked. Well, that's just wrong when thought out loud.

"How old was he?" You think he's angry now. Just wait until he hears this.

"Twenty-five." I watch his knuckles turn white as he strangles the steering wheel. "It's not a big deal. I knew what I was doing."

"There's no way you knew what you were doing at fourteen. It was—"

"Don't, Peter," I warn. I know what it was. I've had years of regret about that night under my belt. I don't need any more guilt forced on me. I stare out the window as I leave California behind little by little. He sighs beside me.

"Okay," he says. "Let's just find something else to talk about."

I close the magazine and toss it onto the back seat. We ride in silence for another half hour.

Peter keeps glancing at me as we hurl down the road toward the mountains. He thinks he's being stealthy about it, but he doesn't realize I can see his reflection in the window. He's been watching me like that for years. At first, I hated it; now, I find I like the attention.

Crossing my legs, I catch when Peter glances at my thighs for a beat before focusing back on the road. I smile to myself when he adjusts in his seat. I've also been able to make him uncomfortably hard for years. Maybe it's the fact I insist on doing everything in the shortest skirts I can get away with. Wait until he sees what I'm hiking in.

"Are we there yet?" I ask in my drollest voice. He smiles like I knew he would. The one thing about Peter and I is we squabble often, but we move on quickly.

"We'll be there in just under an hour."

I sigh dramatically. Rummaging through my bag, I pull out a book to help me pass the time. I bought it specifically for this trip.

"Murder mystery?" he asks.

"It's about a group of campers that are slaughtered on a cross-country hike. More of a thriller."

"Lovely."

"Nothing like a good book to relax me." I flip open my book. Peter's gaze bores into the side of my head. I ignore it and find the chapter I earmarked. Yes, I'm a monster, but I picked the book up at a second-hand store. A little corner bending is the least of its problems. I bought several similar books, planning on leaving them behind as I go.

"Mmmm," he hums, looking back at the road.

"What?" I look up from my book. "No sexual innuendo about relaxing?"

"You know I only do that when Rand is around. Drives him crazy." He smiles. "Seems incredibly inappropriate while we're alone, doesn't it?"

"Mmmm." Now it's my turn to hum.

I've begun to enjoy seeing how he can turn every

comment into something salacious. If any other man said the things Peter has to me, I'd break his face. I just laugh when he does it. I'm sure that is something my therapist should know about. Then again, we all have our secrets.

We drive in silence through the dark until we pull up outside of a small cottage. Peter shuts off the engine, and we climb out. The air is colder here. I feel a shiver work its way through my body as I join him at the front of the SUV. Before I can go hunt for a warmer coat, Peter's arm is draped around my shoulders. I press closer to his warm body.

"What do you think?" he asks. I have so many thoughts swirling in my head. Thoughts of confusion about moving on from what I've ever known. Worry about us making a success of our new business. Fear of not being important to my only brother anymore now that he has his own family.

"Looks promising," is what I say instead. "Shall we check it out?" He motions me forward. He punches in a code on the keypad near the door, and the lock disengages. Inside is an inviting living area with a large fireplace at one end.

"There are two bedrooms; one upstairs, the other down the hall. You can choose which one you want." I walk upstairs to see the first bedroom. It's got large windows that, even though it's currently dark, promise an incredible view. When I return to the living area, Peter has started a fire.

"I'll take the one upstairs." My bags are sitting by the door. How long was I up there?

"I opened a bottle of wine. Help yourself."

Damn. Peter's on his game. I pour myself a glass, toe off my shoes, and sit on the end of the couch. He pokes at the fire for a few more minutes before joining me. Pulling his shoes off, he sets his feet on the coffee table. I tuck my feet underneath me.

"Can I ask you something?" Peter asks after a few minutes.

"Can I stop you?"

"Do you worry we've taken on too much too soon?" he asks, ignoring my comment. It's like he's looked directly into my mind. "I mean, I think we made a good choice, I just...I don't know. I worry that we won't be able to make this work."

He waits for me to say something. But what do I say? Growing up, I learned you never admit your fears. It makes you weak.

"Doesn't matter. There's nowhere else to go but forward at this point," I say, not nearly as confident as I sound.

"Yeah, you're right." He stares at the fire. I wish he'd tell me what else is swirling in that beautiful mind of his. I need him to tell me everything will be alright. I need him to make me forget my fears. "Well, if we're going to get in the Yosemite Valley hike tomorrow, I should probably get some rest."

"Good idea. I would hate for you to slow me down, old man."

I smirk; he smiles.

"I'll see you bright and early." I watch as Peter sets his glass in the sink, closes the screen on the fireplace, and picks up his bag. "Good night, Geneva." With one last look, he walks down the hallway.

"Good night, Peter," I say softly. "Sweet dreams."

PETER

I know Geneva is scared about this move. Even though she won't share her feelings with me, I can see it.

I know more about her than she thinks I do. Like how she fidgets when she's nervous. Or how she becomes unnaturally still when she's angry. How her eyes dilate when I get too close. I'm still working on what that means.

When she's scared, she becomes even more acidic acting than normal. I'm surprised she didn't refer to me by several lady-bit names when I mentioned my concerns about our new business venture.

I pull tomorrow's clothes out of my bag and set them on the dresser. My hiking boots, I set on the floor. I figured Geneva would want to spend the entire day hiking, so I booked this cabin for two nights.

It's been a while since I've been hiking. I'm in good shape, but I have no doubt I'll be sore. I just don't want to disappoint her. I brush my teeth and climb into bed.

I can hear her moving around upstairs. We hang out all the time. I've even stayed at their family home when Rand and I were roommates in school. This is the first time, however, I've ever stayed alone with her.

The shower upstairs turns on and my mind is filled with water rolling down Geneva's naked body. I admit that I've been jacking off to visions of her for years. It's not right. She's my best friend's sister. I've tried pushing her out of my mind to no avail. Even when I've had the occasional girlfriend, they couldn't replace her. And no one-night stand can do her justice.

I slide my hand under the covers and into my boxer briefs. It's the same every time. I start slow as I mentally undress her in my mind. Then I pick up the pace as the action continues from there.

Tonight, however, I don't have to start slow. She's already naked in the shower. My hand begins stroking my hard cock as my mind presses her back against the shower wall.

I imagine Geneva likes it rough, so I waste no time lifting her up so she can wrap her legs around me. My fist squeezes as I push inside her in one thrust. She gasps, but I don't give her any quarter. I drive my hips forward in punishing strokes. She tries to close her eyes, but I demand they stay on me. I want to see them when she comes.

It never takes long. She's too perfect for me to last. My spine tingles as she undulates on top of me. She uses her thighs to work me exactly how I like it. My hands squeeze her ass, encouraging her to speed up. I'm so close.

She moans, and I can't hold on any longer. Hot cum squirts over my hand. I sigh. Once again, I'm left wishing for more.

I climb out of bed to clean up. The water upstairs is off. I stare up at the ceiling, wondering what she's wearing. Doesn't matter; she's still my best friend's sister. She's still so far out of my reach, she's untouchable. I lay back down and continue staring at the ceiling.

If she wasn't Rand's sister, would I make a play for her? I doubt it. She's too far out of my league. She's beautiful, but terrifying. It takes a long time to get to know the real her. She rarely lets down her walls.

I know she's as beautiful on the inside as she is on the outside. But I only see it because of the years I've been friends with Rand. It's why she never has a boyfriend. And why she cared so little about her virginity that she gave it away so young.

I roll over on my side. I've got to get my mind off of her for tonight. I'm exhausted from everything that's been happening. I've got to get some sleep.

I want to be my best tomorrow. I get to spend the entire day with her and I want it to be perfect. And like every night since I was a boy, I drift off with visions of Geneva sifting through my mind.

three

PETER

"GOOD MORNING," I greet Geneva when she arrives downstairs bright and early the next morning. She's wearing a pair of athletic leggings, a tank top, and wool socks. She sets her shoes by mine at the back door.

"Something smells good," she says, sliding onto one of the barstools.

"I thought we could use something good to eat before heading out." It's still dark outside, so we have time.

I set a large bowl of oatmeal in front of her. She loads it up with cream, brown sugar, raisins, walnuts, and cinnamon. I scoop out some fruit from a container. When the English muffins are toasted, I add butter.

"Did you think to buy food for the trail?" she asks between bites.

"On the table, waiting to be packed."

She spins around to look at the food I organized on the coffee table before turning back around. "Nailing it, Peter."

It takes everything in my power not to turn that statement into something obscene.

"What? Nothing?"

"Behave, Geneva," I growl. She rolls her eyes.

We finish our breakfast quickly. I know she's anxious to get on the trails. When our packs are loaded and we're layered properly, we drive to Glacier Point.

There are several cars in the lot, but no one is around. I suspect we're between the diehard hikers and the recreational ones. We shrug into our backpacks. Geneva has a rare smile on her face.

"Lead on," I say, handing her the GPS.

She strides toward the trail. I have to move quickly to keep from getting left behind. She sets a punishing pace. By the time she finally stops at Illilouette Falls, I've realized I'm not in as good a shape as I think. The two-and-a-half miles down the mountain feels more like fifteen.

"Wow," she whispers. That makes the blisters threatening my feet all worth it. "Have you ever seen anything like it?" She grins at me, and my knees grow weak.

"Never," I agree. I'm not talking about the scenery. Her cheeks are pink, her eyes are shining when she looks at me, and I've never seen anything better than Geneva with a smile.

"Why haven't we done this before? What were we thinking?" she asks with a laugh.

"I guess we weren't." I pull out my phone and snap a couple of pictures with her in them. She's even in a good enough mood to agree to a selfie. Must be the lack of oxygen.

"Ready?" She starts back down the trail before I can protest, and I fall in step behind her.

The trail to Nevada Falls is longer and full of switchbacks. We meet another pair of hikers going in the opposite direction up the mountain. They must be insane. Downhill is hard enough. After a quick greeting, we continue toward the falls.

Geneva veers off the trail after a series of switchbacks. The path is unmarked, but she acts like she knows where she's going, so I follow. I have to give her credit, the view is amazing.

We decide to eat something in a clearing just big enough for us to sit down. I pull out a pack of tuna I see her eat at the office. There's trail mix, mandarin oranges, peanut butter crackers, and cubes of cheese.

"You're good at this," she says, scooping out the tuna. If she could see my legs shaking, she wouldn't say that. "We should do this more often."

"Maybe we'll have more time now to take some time off." I offer her the trail mix. She takes a handful.

"Do you think Rand would want to come?"

"I think so." The hint of uncertainty concerns me. Geneva is nothing if not self-assured. It hasn't occurred to me until now that Rand's new life might be having more of an impact on her than I realized.

"I bet Brontë will be onboard also," I continue. "We should plan something for the four of us in a couple of months. Maybe a trip to Big Bend to check out that park."

"We should probably keep going," she says after considering my suggestion in silence for a moment.

"Are you sure we don't want to take the Muir Trail? I read it's not quite as steep."

"Come on, Peter." Standing, she helps me up. "Don't be such a pussy."

There's the Geneva I know. We rejoin the main trail and continue on. We hike through small streams and switchbacks until we eventually reach Nevada Falls. She insists we take the footbridge for a bird's-eye view of the falls. More photos, a quick snack, and off we go.

We reach the Mist Trail, and I get a good look at the steep rock staircase we have to descend. I would really like to turn around. We should turn around, but Geneva is excited about pushing us past what I believe we're capable of. We start our descent slowly, picking our way down the rocks.

I know why they call it the Mist Trail. A gentle mist adds to the treachery of the descent, making the rocks wet. We should have turned around. I'm standing higher on the trail trying to catch my breath for a minute when it happens.

One moment, she's on her feet, heading down. The next, she goes down, and there's nothing I can do to stop it. She cries out as she slides several feet down the rocks. My heart leaps into my throat. I can't tell how far she's fallen.

"Geneva!" I yell, throwing off my backpack. I scramble down as carefully as possible with my heart thundering in my chest. I kneel next to her. Her face is scrunched in pain.

"Where are you hurt?" My hands seem to have a mind of their own as they touch every inch of her body for injuries. She finally slaps them away. Weirdly, it's comforting.

"My ankle," she says between gritted teeth. I move so I can access her ankle. I can already see it swelling inside her boot.

"I don't want to take your boot off. If it's broken, I could do even more damage."

She nods her head.

"Do you think you can put weight on it?"

She nods again. Carefully, I help her stand, but the second she puts weight on her left foot, she cries out.

"It's fine, it's fine," I mumble. I think I'm trying to assure myself as much as her. "Sit back down."

I ease her back to the ground. Climbing back up the trail, I retrieve my backpack. I have to figure out how I'm going to get us down to the bottom. There's no way I can haul us both back up the way we came. Sitting next to her, I dig through my pack.

"Here, take these," I say, shaking some anti-inflammatories into my hand. She takes them without arguing. "I'm going to secure some ice around it." I pull out two small ice packs, break them to start them getting cold and ease them into the sides of her boot. Then I pull out compression wrap and secure the entire ankle in it.

"How are you doing?" I pull off her sunglasses and watch her pupils dilate. That's a good sign.

"I've been better," she says, snatching her sunglasses back. That's an even better sign. "You should keep going and send someone back for me."

"Nope." I don't know how I'll get her down, but I'm not leaving her here. "I'm not leaving you here."

"Pete—"

"I said no." I'm not wasting time listening to her argue with me. We're going down together. I look at what we have to work with. It's not much. "Can you wear your pack?" She nods.

I move everything important I can into her pack. She slides it on her shoulders, and I leave mine next to the trail. If we're lucky, someone will find it and bring it down.

"Okay, let's go."

She whimpers when I pull her off the ground. I brace myself on the rocks and have her hop onto my back. She whimpers again but quickly stifles it. I know how much pain she's in. I had a behemoth midfielder land on my ankle playing lacrosse in school, and they had to haul my butt off the field.

"You need to be as still as possible so I don't lose my balance. This is going to take a while. If you need a rest, you have to let me know. We'll stop." I take a step down, and she tenses. "You trust me, don't you?"

"Yes."

"Then trust me to get you down." I slowly begin fighting my way down the mountain. My foot lowers to the next step. Her grip tightens around my shoulders. I can feel her puff out a breath every time my boot connects to the next rock.

I've made it halfway when I slip on some loose stones. We slide for a second before I can regain my balance.

"We're fine, G. I've got you," I reassure both of us.

"I know," she whispers against my ear. "I trust you."

I continue down until the trail evens out again. My knees buckle as I try to ease her to the ground. She scrambles off my back before I can recover. She swings her pack around to pull out the canteen. Gratefully, I take it.

"You can still leave me here and get help," she argues. "I'll be fine."

"I'm not arguing with you. We stay together. I don't want to leave you to the bears. If we're together, they're sure to eat me first. They always go for the ugliest first. You can get away."

I'm joking. I don't want to be eaten by a bear any more than the next person. But I'm rewarded with a slight smile from Geneva, which is what I was aiming for.

"That's stupid. Even I know you're too beautiful to be

eaten first." Her face reddens slightly, and she looks at the ground. "I think you are anyway."

"We should probably keep going." I don't know what to think about her statement. She's never said anything like it before. Does she think I'm beautiful? Shock must be setting in.

I help her back up and secure her pack on her back again. Bending, I wait until she's firmly settled on my back before starting. It's a matter of putting one foot in front of the other now.

A hike that should have taken us around seven hours takes us closer to eleven. I have to set her down several times to rest. Her ankle looks worse every time we stop. We're saved when two rangers with flashlights find us a mile from the end of the trail.

"Hey, there. You must be our missing hikers. We found your vehicle at the other end and decided we'd better find you," one of them says. I didn't catch their names, I'm too focused on how ecstatic I am to finally get some help.

"Good thing we did," the other one says. They ease Geneva off my back, each man taking a side. Slowly, they help her back to the trailhead. They load her into one of their vehicles and head toward the nearest emergency room. The other ranger takes me back to our vehicle.

"I don't know how you hauled her down the Mist Trail like that," the ranger says. "Usually people just leave the injured party where they are and hike out to find help. During the busy season, they just wait for someone to come along. She must really be something to hike that far with her on your back."

"She's my best friend's sister. I couldn't just leave her. He would kill me."

"Whatever you need to tell yourself." I ignore the grin

he throws at me. "Well, here we are." He pulls up next to my SUV and gives me directions to the emergency room. I throw Geneva's pack inside.

Spinning out of the parking area, I speed toward town. It's a half hour before I reach the hospital.

"Geneva Randolph, please," I ask the woman at the desk. She waves me to a row of curtains. I walk quickly down the row until I find her propped up in one of the beds. "Hey, how's the ankle?"

"Well, it's not broken," an older man in a lab coat walking up says. He's carrying an iPad in his hands. "The good news is, it's just sprained. A couple of days of ice and rest should have you going again. Leave it wrapped until tomorrow, then I suggest you invest in a brace." He tosses one on the bed. "Use an anti-inflammatory as needed." He nods at us and walks off down the hall.

"Okay. I'd guess bedside manners are not his strong suit," I say.

"Whatever. Just help me out of here." She hops off the table and grimaces. I wrap my arm under her, grab the brace, and we awkwardly hobble out from behind the curtain. We stop at the desk for her to sign some paperwork.

My car is right out front where I left it. I was too concerned about Geneva to bother finding a parking spot. Fortunately, it's late enough that no one has towed it off.

"Are you hungry?" I ask after settling her in the passenger side.

"I am, but can you just make something at the cabin? I'm more desperate for a shower than food. And I'm supposed to prop my stupid foot up."

"Here, let me have your foot." She looks at me like I'm crazy. "Let me have your foot." She rolls her eyes but scoots around in the seat until her foot is resting on my leg. I slide the Land Rover into gear. "What would you like to eat?"

"Anything. I could eat that fabled bear you mentioned at this point. But more french toast would not go untouched."

"Whatever you'd like," I say with a grin. It's what she always wants if she's had a bad day. "It wasn't all bad, was it?" She considers me for a beat.

"It was amazing up until my stupidity. Even then, the scenery was still beautiful." She laughs. "And I got to see Peter Winsloe hulk out like a badass. Nothing could top that."

four

GENEVA

THE NIGHT WAS ROUGH. Peter insisted I sleep in his bedroom while he slept on the couch. Just in case I needed anything. It was a nice gesture, but being surrounded by sheets that smell like Peter made for a long night. It quite possibly could have been what led to several fantasy dreams he starred in.

At least my ankle is feeling a little better. I push to a sitting position and try putting weight on it. Yep, still tender. Carefully, I stand on one leg. Hopping into the living room, I find him sitting on the couch with a far-off look in his eyes. If I didn't know better, I'd swear he's hungover.

"What's up?" I ask, joining him on the couch. He slowly swings his head to look at me.

"I think I'm broken."

"How so?"

"I can barely move. My muscles are screaming." That sounds a bit melodramatic, but who am I to judge?

"Okay. When do we have to check out?"

"Whenever. The guy said he doesn't have anyone coming in behind us so we can take as much time as we want. I don't think it's a bad idea to stay an extra night if we want. I can push everything a day."

"We'll see. Here's what we're going to do for now though. You get naked; I'm running you a bath." I stand on one leg and hold my hand out to pull him up. He studies it for a minute before shrugging and taking it. It takes a few minutes, but between our combined efforts, he finally makes it upright.

"After you get out of the tub, wrap a towel around your waist and lay down on the bed. I have something that will help with the soreness."

Peter must truly be in a lot of pain because he doesn't even argue with me. He follows me into the bathroom. Stripping down to his underwear (which takes an act of Congress), he waits while I add Epsom salts to the bath. He stares at the water.

"Do you need help getting in?" I ask.

"I'm good." He pushes off the wall.

"Okay. Be careful, I made the water pretty hot. But you need to soak for a while. The salt should help draw some of the soreness out."

"I know what Epsom salts do."

"Fine, grouch. I'll be outside." I close the bathroom door behind me and try not to imagine Peter in all his glory. I've seen him plenty of times in nothing more than a swimming suit, but never au naturel. Not that we need to be prancing around naked in front of each other. That would certainly bring a whole new dimension to this road trip.

I hear him groan as he sits in the tub. I need to get out of here. Nothing good can come from hovering outside the bathroom while fantasizing about him in the tub.

Breakfast should keep me occupied for a little while. Hopping into the kitchen, I find cereal and milk. Normally, nothing passes my lips that isn't either healthy or made by Peter. I'll just have to make an exception this morning. I don't think either of us is in any shape to cook. No one would want to eat my cooking anyway.

By the time he rises from the tub, I'm back sitting on the bed. I've already dug my bar of muscle rub out of my bag. We'll both smell like old men shortly.

Peter emerges from the bathroom with a towel wrapped low around his waist. I pat the bed next to me and he lays down on his stomach with the towel still covering him.

"You're not going to beat me with twigs or something else equally ridiculous, are you?" he asks, and I roll my eyes. It's lost on him though since he's face down in the pillows.

I don't deem to answer him. Instead, I carefully straddle his legs. My ankle protests a little, but nothing I can't handle. His mumbling turns into moans when I begin to work the bar over his neck and shoulders.

When he's good and greased up, I use my hands to knead the muscles. Every time he winces, I work that area a little more. I make it to the small of his back eventually. There's not a lot I can do here with the towel. Grabbing it with both hands, I work it out from under him.

"What are you doing?" he complains. "Give me that." He makes a lunge for the towel. Not easy while lying on your stomach.

"It's not like I haven't seen it before."

"Not mine," he points out. Managing to snatch the towel back, he throws it over his ass.

"How am I going to get to your glutes?"

"Your hands don't need to be on my glutes. They'll just have to work themselves out. They're fine."

That's one thing we can both agree on; they are fine. I've admired those glutes hiding under his pants for quite a while now. From the brief glance I got, they did not disappoint. I run my hands under the towel, pressing against his perfect ass. He groans.

"How do you have such a smooth ass?"

"Geneva."

"What? It's a legitimate question." I knead his glutes harder this time. He forgets he should be protesting. I know what it took to carry me down the mountain. They have to be killing him. "I'd sort of like to bite them."

"Jesus, Geneva." Pushing up on his forearms, he looks over his shoulder at me. "Just keep your hands out from under the towel."

"Scared you won't like it?" Fine, I'm taunting him. It's fun though.

"I'm scared I would. So, hands off the goods."

"Can I at least give it a good spanking?"

Peter lets out an exasperated snort and collapses back among the pillows. Does that mean I can? I laugh to myself. He's good at dishing it out; not so great at taking it.

"What if I let you spank mine first?" I tease.

"Don't tempt me," he mumbles.

I laugh again and slide down his legs. I don't think I've ever felt tighter hamstrings. You could bounce a quarter off of these suckers.

"Oww," he complains.

This time, I do smack his perfect ass. He jerks slightly. But I'm back working on his legs before he can protest.

"Stop whining," I say. "Or I'll give you something to whine about."

"What else could you possibly do that's worse than getting spanked?" he mumbles around the pillows.

"You'd be surprised."

He rolls on his back suddenly and sits up. Sadly, he's very adept at keeping the towel positioned over his crown jewels. That's fine, I'm more of a hip lady myself, and there's plenty of it showing around the towel. I would sigh, but he's staring at me like I've grown a second head. His mouth opens like he wants to ask a question, but he reconsiders before he does.

"Lie down on your back so your head is at this end of the bed. I'll work on your shoulders and pecs," I say.

He considers me a moment more before shrugging his shoulders. He winces at the soreness but lies down. Eyes the color of the ocean stare up at me as I rub the ointment bar over his pecs. They slowly close as my hands meet warm skin. I trace over the muscles with my knuckles the way my massage therapist does. His breathing grows shallow.

"I don't think this is a good idea," he growls.

"Just pretend I'm some big sweaty guy working on you."

"You'll never be big and sweaty. More like a temptress in spandex."

My hands freeze on his chest. Looking down at his face, I find he's watching me again. It would be so easy to kiss him.

"Don't," he says like he's read my mind. "I won't want to stop."

"Would it be so bad?" I know what he's going to say, but I don't let him get the words out. Will anything hurt as much as having my heart broken by Peter? I know I don't want to find out. Before he can say anything more, I leave the room. I just take my hands off his chest and flee as fast as I can with a bum ankle.

"Geneva!" he calls after me.

I don't wait. I hop one leg at a time up the steps to the bedroom with my stuff. We should move on as soon as possible. I'll pack my stuff and we can go.

"Geneva?" he says, stepping into the room. I do a double take at him in nothing. The only thing providing any privacy is the towel he holds strategically in front of him.

"I think we should head to Zion. There's no reason to stay here." My eyes refocus on the bed. I throw my Dopp kit into my duffel.

"Okay." He stands in the middle of the room, waiting for more. I can't take a chance on telling him more. There are only two men in this world capable of breaking me. Peter is one. If I don't let him in, then he can't touch me.

We'll get to Austin. He'll go one way, and I'll go the other. Soon, I'll find some pretty boy southern charmer to hook up with. Peter will be nothing more than my business partner. And if you believe that, I have some lovely beachfront property in Arizona you might be interested in.

"I'll take your bag down," he says, wrapping the towel around his waist.

He takes the bag from my hand. His strong arms help me back down the stairs. Every moment he touches me is agony. When he leaves me on the couch to dress, I shiver. Not because I'm cold, but because I miss his heat. I can't really explain it. It just is.

"Let me load the car. I'll come back for you." He picks up the bags and disappears outside. I've turned this into something awkward. "Ready?" he asks, stepping back inside.

I nod. He picks me up in his arms and carries me to the car. Carefully, he places me in the passenger seat.

"I'll lock up and be right back." The door closes with a resounding slam.

He stomps back up the steps to the door. His body language speaks volumes. He's angry. I stare out the windshield as he slides into the driver's side. We leave the cabin behind for the next adventure. We drive in silence for half an hour.

"I think we should make some rules," he says finally. "Just so we keep things on a friendly basis from here on." This should be good. "So there's no misunderstandings."

"Go on," I say. Crossing my legs, I turn to glare at him. He used to shrink from my glares. Now, I think he enjoys them. I can't wait to hear what rules he thinks I'm going to abide by.

"First, no partial nudity. No walking around in towels or underwear. That's my fault." He glances at me. "Absolutely no body massages going forward. I do feel much better though. Thank you. But I'll just be sore next time."

"Is that it?"

"No sexual innuendos. That's also on me. It's not appropriate when we're alone. Also, no more surveys or articles about sex. Just leave *Cosmo* in the back seat from here on."

"So no talking, touching, or reading?" I ask. "Is that what you're saying?"

"You know what I'm saying. Nothing that hints at us having sex or thinking about having sex. No friends with benefits or fuck buddies or whatever you want to call it."

"Damn, you sure have sex on the brain, Peter," I tease.

He cuts a frustrated look at me. I imagine just talking about us not having sex has him hard. The poor man doesn't realize he just threw the gauntlet down.

"Hmm," I say, tapping at my bottom lip with a fingernail. This might be a way to separate my feelings for him from my lust. If I can do that, we'll both win.

"Geneva," he warns.

"What?"

"The rules. Don't you think they're a good idea? You agree, right?" He glances at me again. There's worry etched in the space between his eyebrows. He should be worried. I'm debating how badly I'm going to shred those rules into tiny pieces. "Geneva?"

"They're certainly something."

"But you agree, right?"

"More or less."

"Fuck me," he breathes as his hand runs through his hair.

Yes, Mr. Winsloe, that's exactly what I was thinking.

five

GENEVA

I THINK I really did break Peter. He keeps giving me nervous side-eyes. He's always been a little leery around me, but this is beyond that. Does he really think I'll jump him in the middle of the California desert? Will I?

It's not a bad plan. But not when he looks like he's about to bolt. This is more of a game of cat and mouse, and I need to sharpen my claws first.

"How are you feeling?" I ask to break the silence. "Sore?"

"A little. How's your ankle?"

"Same," I admit. Some of the swelling is gone, but a nasty bruise wraps around it.

"Let me have your foot." I move my foot to his lap. "Maybe if it stays elevated, it'll help." His hand mindlessly traces over the bruise. I don't hate the feeling. He has large, strong hands that never fail to render me into jelly when they touch me.

"Hang on, let me grab something to entertain us."

Pulling my foot out of his lap, I swing onto my knees to peer into the back seat. I grab some of the magazines and puzzle books before falling back into the passenger seat. Peter's gripping the steering wheel so tight his knuckles are white. Yeah, I know what my ass in his face does to him.

"Okay there?" He ignores me, and I slide my foot back into his lap. He lays his hand on it, continuing the slow circles. I doubt he even realizes what he's doing.

"Here we go," I say, opening the first magazine on my lap. "Do you have a type?" I flip to the page number of the survey. I bet he throws this copy of *Cosmo* into the trash next time we stop.

"Type of what?" he asks.

"Good try. First question." He groans. "Do you use dating to find what you want in a partner or what you don't want?"

"I..." He stops to think about the question. "I don't know. I've gone on dates where we had nothing to talk about and some where it was all just talk. I didn't find either woman physically desirable. That makes me sound horrible, doesn't it?"

"No, I get it. So do you want her to be similar to you or different?"

"Different. I think I'd get bored if she were just like me. I already have two sisters that are similar to me, I don't want a partner that is also. They do say opposites attract. Just so she's not so different that I can't relate to anything in her life."

"Interesting," I say. "Is that why your apartment is a revolving door of women?"

"Believe it or not, I'm not the manwhore that my reputation suggests. I think Rand started those rumors to make me more interesting."

"One of the people in HR told me that the first time. I heard you had a three-way." Even I know that one was totally fabricated, but why not throw that out there to see if he bites?

"From who?" He stares at me in horror. For a moment, I worry we'll wreck. He shakes his head and returns his attention back to the road. "That's ridiculous."

"Is it though?" He glares at me again, so I move on. "So do you have a list of deal breakers or must-haves?"

"Do you?" he asks.

"Absolutely. It occupies several volumes."

"Such as?"

"To start, he has to be taller than I am. It's not fair, but there it is. I also don't like bro guys that still act like they're at an endless frat party even though they're in their forties. But I don't want an asshole billionaire who believes the world revolves around him. No sports fanatics. I can do an occasional Sunday football game, but I'm not doing every date night eating wings in a bar."

"That's quite the list." He smiles at me.

"There's more. He can't live with his mom unless she's elderly and infirm. No fast food or movies on the first date. He has to own a vehicle, pay for the first date, and no farting during sex."

"Damn. What if it just sneaks out?"

"Deal-breaker. I'm not fooling myself; I know he's going to fart all the time when we get married. There's no reason to start early in the relationship."

He laughs. I have to join in. It is kind of a ridiculous list.

"What about must-haves?"

"I've already said he has to be taller," I say. "He has to have manners. Chewing with his mouth open is also a deal-breaker. Open doors, shit like that. Absolutely has to be employed in a career that requires some ambition. Oh, and he also has to worship the ground I walk on."

Peter laughs again. He pulls into the parking lot of a diner. Stopping in a parking place near the door, he turns off the SUV.

"How about some lunch, your grace?"

"Now you're getting the hang of it."

Lunch turns out to be better than the exterior of the building would suggest. I order a vegan wrap that includes ample avocado. Peter gets a burger with everything. We continue our discussion from the car at length until our food arrives. The conclusion we come to is this: Peter has no type, and I like, well, men like Peter. I didn't really need a quiz to tell me that.

"How much farther do we have to drive?" I ask, stretching beside the car. My body is starting to protest missing my daily workout.

"We're not even to Bakersfield yet. It'll be dark by the time we make it to Vegas."

"Did you say Vegas?" Did my ears deceive me? I could swear he mentioned the most sinfully awesome playground in the western United States. I've gotten into so much trouble in Las Vegas in the past it's a wonder I'm still alive. But I'll never tell. What happens there stays there, as did the bendy circus acrobat I hooked up with once.

"I thought we'd stay a couple of nights. Recoup from our climb."

"What a brilliant idea." It's all I can do to stop myself from rubbing my hands together in glee. My mind starts spinning with all the possibilities of things we can do. "Do you want me to drive for a while?"

"I'm good, but thanks."

He climbs into the SUV, and I join him, placing my foot in his lap once again.

I wonder how good Peter is at gambling. He has a brilliant mind for numbers, so there's a chance we could leave Vegas richer than when we arrived. Our best bet is in the high rollers area. It costs more to buy in, but the profits are also much larger.

"Do you mind if I close my eyes for a little while?" I'm going to need to rest up if I'm going to make it tonight. There will be no time once we hit town.

I've got to secure us appropriate clothes, apply for the high roller area, and convince Peter to play. The latter shouldn't be hard to do. I have just the cut of dress in mind to convince him.

"Of course not. Here." He reaches behind him and pulls a pillow and blanket from somewhere. The man really does think of everything. Ten bucks says he was a Boy Scout. I search my mind for any memory of him in a khaki uniform when we were young. All I remember is the private school uniform he looked delicious in.

Curling up on the seat, I pull the blanket up to my chin. Soft music starts on the radio as I drift off. Tonight is going to be epic.

* * *

PETER

Geneva really is beautiful when she sleeps. I know that sounds creepy. The first time I watched her sleep, we were fifteen and fourteen. Her father had flown into a rage over something Rand had supposedly done. I was visiting over break at the time. We fled into the boathouse to hide and wound up staying all night.

I was so terrified he'd find us that I stayed awake. It was the first time I saw him strike my best friend. It's something I've never forgotten. When Rand went to work for him after college, I followed him. The thought of their father continuing to terrorize them was more than I could let pass. I've hovered around ever since.

As far as I know, Geneva's father has never struck her. I would kill him if he did. Instead, most of his wrath was saved for his son. He didn't know what to do with me when I stepped between them.

My brother said I was too invested in their welfare. But what else could I do? My family didn't act like that. I couldn't walk away from that situation.

It took a lot of convincing to talk Geneva into leaving her father's company. I think she held to the conviction that the devil you know is better than the unknown. She needs to embrace the unknown.

She's too smart to be relegated to the sidelines where her father thought she belonged just because she was born female. Geneva can do anything she sets her mind to. Usually better than the rest of us.

I'm a little worried about the gleam in her eyes when I mentioned stopping in Las Vegas. I know she's spent several long weekends there over the years. I try not to think about what mischief she got into. Or what mischief she plans for us. Whatever is swirling in that pretty head of hers will be outrageous. With any luck, there will be no tigers or face tattoos involved.

We travel like this for miles. She's stretched across the front with her feet resting in my lap. Her dark hair is in a braid that reaches to the small of her back. Her small hands are tucked under her cheek. They can be lethal in the sparring ring when they need to.

Her legs are encased in skin-tight leggings. They go on for miles when she's dressed up for a formal event. In the sky-high heels she wears, she's almost my height.

"Are you watching me?" she asks in a sleepy voice.

"Just checking on you."

"You're always checking on me." She rearranges her pillow. "Ever since we were in the boathouse."

"I didn't think you'd remember that."

"How can I not?" I tuck the blanket tighter over her feet. "Pressed between you and Rand, it was the first time I felt truly safe."

She drifts back to sleep, and I focus on the road in front of me. If I don't, I might pull over and drag her into my lap. That's all I've ever wanted for her. To feel safe. Happy. It's why Rand trusts me to take care of her. We want the same thing.

The miles tick away under us. With each mile, I fall harder for Geneva. How can I not? A hole opens in my heart that I wish she could fill. But her trust in me has to come at a price. I can't lose what we have. My friendship with her and her brother is too sacred to mess up.

"Hey, sweetheart. We're almost there," I say, rousing her from sleep. We're on the outskirts of Las Vegas.

"Really?" She stretches her arms above her head. A thin strip of skin between her shirt and leggings captures my attention. "How long was I out?"

"A couple of hours."

"I must have really needed some rest," she says. "All the packing wore me out, I guess." She sits up as we roll through the suburbs. "I love the lights."

The lights are about the only thing I like about this

town, although I've never spent much time here. I grew up in a small town in Virginia. Las Vegas was always just a fictional world on television. Rand insisted we spend my twenty-first birthday here, but it wasn't for me. All the drinking and lap dances just left me feeling empty.

Not that I'm a prude. I like to drink and dance as much as the next guy. In moderation. Too much of anything isn't fun. I woke up the morning after my birthday in a strange place with a strange person. It was my first and last walk of shame.

"I can't wait to see where we're staying," Geneva says, interrupting my thoughts. "I hope you're up for an adventure."

"Why? What do you have in mind?"

"Nothing you can't handle." She smiles. "Don't worry, Peter. I'll be gentle on you."

That's what worries me most. Vicious Geneva I can handle. Gentle Geneva? I've not seen that side very often. It terrifies me. I just pray there are no random babies involved.

"You know we still have to be in Austin in a week, right?" I ask.

"You worry too much." She shakes her head. "Austin's a world away. I say live in the moment."

Lord, help me.

six

PETER

WHEN I DECIDED Las Vegas would be a good place to recharge after climbing in Yosemite, I must have been out of my mind. I booked two nights and two rooms in one of the nicer casinos.

That was before Geneva fell down the mountain. Her ankle is still swollen, and a bruise wraps around it. I know this because her foot has been in my lap for the last seven hours. She keeps insisting that it's fine. I don't believe that for a second.

We pull onto the strip, and her eyes immediately light up. She's almost vibrating with excitement. This doesn't bode well for me for the next forty-eight hours.

I'm already a little worried she's scheming how to break every single one of the rules I established. They don't seem unreasonable. No nudity, sexual innuendos, or discussions involving sex should keep me away from Rand's little sister. Right?

"I love the lights," she says again.

"It is something to see."

"It's like the beacon to debauchery."

"We're not here long enough for debauchery," I say with a scowl.

"There's time for a little debauchery." She holds her fingers, almost touching them together, to prove her point. She's in for a shock though. If I don't get to see her naked, no one else does either. "Where are we staying?"

"Right here." I pull the SUV into the Venetian. The valet meets us to whisk our bags inside. Handing the keys to the SUV over, I follow Geneva inside.

I've been inside the hotel several times when business brought Rand and me to Nevada, but I've never stayed here. The cost of a room always felt too extravagant for me. Until Geneva came along anyway.

"I'm going to shop a little while you check in," she says.

I watch as she walks toward the Grand Canal shops. She seems to already know her way around, and that worries me. I turn my attention away from her when a pleasant woman asks if I'm checking in.

I've been in and out of so many hotels over the years, I can do this in my sleep. Checking in is easy; finding Geneva in the throng of shoppers is a different matter.

It doesn't take me long to give up the hunt, and I find a restaurant with a seating area in the mall and wait for a table. They sit me on the railing by the foot traffic so I can watch for her to drift by. I'm sure she'll be better at locating me than vice versa. The waitress brings me a beer, and I settle in.

My phone vibrates in my front pocket. It's Rand checking on our progress. I'm filling him in on our adventure so far, minus the twisted ankle, when I feel someone slip into the seat next to mine. I was right. Her hunting instincts are much better than mine.

"We must stop meeting like this," Geneva drawls. "What will my husband think?" Her eyes twinkle with mischief. She's so beautiful. For just a moment, I think about throwing the rules out the window. Then I finish my text to her brother. Our friendship is why there are rules in the first place.

"He'll think he's a very lucky man to have married you. Even if he has to share."

She throws her head back and laughs. Her throat is a long column of soft skin that begs to be kissed. Her soft jade gaze meets mine. I pick up the menu. "Is this place fine for dinner?"

"Of course," she says, picking up her menu. "How's the beer?"

"Not bad." She picks up my glass and throws back a mouthful.

"I'll have one of these and the chicken Caesar, dressing on the side," she tells our waitress. She waits for me to order before continuing. "All the french toast is going to make me fat." I know she's teasing, but I can't stop the scowl that crosses my face.

"I doubt that," I snarl. "Who cares if it did? You'd still be stunning."

"Why, Peter Winsloe, are you trying to seduce me?"

"No seducing, remember." I roll my eyes. "I'm just stating a fact."

The waitress sets Geneva's beer on the table. She takes a long pull before turning her attention back to me. Her eyes narrow.

"I don't remember anything in the rules about seduction," she says.

"It's understood. It's between nakedness and innuendo."

"That only applies to us though. I can play naked Twister in my room with anyone else of my choosing. Isn't that right?"

"I guess. Technically." She's teasing me. I hope anyway. The idea of her playing naked anything with someone else makes me see red.

I'm saved from saying something I might regret by the waitress. She delivers the salad and my nachos. Geneva immediately steals one from my plate like I knew she would.

"I forgot to tell you, I'm having something delivered to your room." She picks up her fork and spears a bite of lettuce. "For later."

"What's happening later?" I ask.

"We're in Vegas. We're going out."

"What about your ankle?"

"Peter," she says, shaking her head. "I get hurt a lot sparring at my academy. I heal quickly, and you've got it wrapped so well I barely feel it. It'll be good for a night."

We finish our meal and head to our rooms. They're on the same floor but several doors apart. I agree to meet her in the lobby in forty-five minutes, which gives me just enough time for a shower and change into fresh clothes.

When I open my room door, I find a suit bag lying on the couch, and inside is a black tuxedo. The matching shoes sit next to the coffee table. I can't imagine what she has in mind for tonight, but I'll play along.

I stop in the bedroom area just long enough to pull my shaving kit out of my duffel. The bathroom is larger than the one I left in San Francisco. It boasts a riot of marble and brass. There's a standing shower that I'm looking forward to.

Stripping out of my road-weary clothes, I step into water just barely below scalding. The showerhead is tall enough that I don't have to stoop to wash my hair. That can be an issue when you're six feet two.

I hope Geneva's room is as nice as mine. I wonder if she's also in the shower and getting ready. The image of water running down her soaped body makes my cock jerk.

Do I have time to jerk off? Do I dare not to and fight all night to keep my cock under control? If I'm wearing a tux, she must be dressing in something slinky. That thought makes it stand at full attention.

For the sake of my own sanity, I lather up my hand before wrapping it around my aching erection. My body knows exactly what to do. It's done this so many times after spending the day at work around her.

My fist slides up and down, tightening with every stroke. It takes nothing more than my imagination conjuring her body writhing under mine for hot lava to race through my system. It covers my hand and the shower floor.

I rinse myself clean, then turn the faucet to the coldest setting. When I begin to shiver, I turn the water off. Hopefully between rubbing one out and the ice shower, I'll survive the night.

I throw a towel around my waist. Staring at myself in the mirror, I debate my facial hair. I've been thinking about shaving it clean for a while. This seems like the perfect time to do so. New start; new look.

When I'm done, I look at my face. Not too bad. Same square jaw I had as a teenager. Fortunately, though, I no longer look like a teenager. That was the reason I grew a beard in the first place. I wonder if Geneva will approve? I guess I'll find out soon.

She is chronically late to everything. That's why I assume I'll have to wait downstairs until she drifts in. I'm more than a little surprised to find her waiting for me this time. She's in a long red dress with a slit up the side that shows off one long tanned leg. This image is even better than the fantasy in the shower. She spots me from across the room.

"Let me see," she says when I reach her. She takes my chin in one hand. She looks back and forth from one side of my face to the other. "It's been so long since I've seen this face. You still have a jaw that can cut glass." She pushes up to her toes and nips at it.

"I miss this face," she whispers. I take in the smell of jasmine that lingers on her skin for a beat or two. Then I ease her away from me.

"What are we doing this well-dressed?" I ask to redirect us.

"Gambling, of course," she answers. "Bond style."

"I think Bond gambled in Monte Carlo," I point out.

"I know, but anything worth doing is worth doing well," she says. "Besides, look how fabulous we look." She steps in front of me and points to a mirror. She's right. With her back pressed against me, we look amazing. Well, she looks amazing. I look like a guy who is desperate for her attention.

I never wear a tuxedo. There's never a reason to. Rand was always the face of the business. I'm happier remaining in the background at my drafting table.

My parents weren't wealthy. I've never learned the refinement that Rand and Geneva possess. The only reason I was even at boarding school with Rand was because of a scholarship. While most of the other students treated me as less than, Rand never seemed to see a difference between us.

"Don't we look stunning?" she asks.

"You always look stunning," I answer.

She smiles at me over her shoulder. Taking my hand, she pulls me through the lobby to the casino. We bypass the normal games being played by normal people. Her mind is set on the high roller room.

A man at the entrance checks her name before welcoming us inside. She was a busy girl while I was dressing.

"What do you want to play first?" I ask.

"Craps, of course." She greets the server and orders a martini. I request a club soda. One of us needs to make sure we don't lose all of our money tonight. "Okay, Mr. Winsloe. Let's see what you're made of." Chips are slid across the table as I find a place at the rail. Geneva is immediately invited to roll the dice.

I place my bet, and the dealer calls for the roll. Geneva tosses the dice. It's not a seven or eleven, but we're not sunk either. A nine works as long as she rolls it again. She throws the dice again to the end of the table. I actually win some money this time. We continue for a while as my chips grow taller slowly.

She becomes bored soon. I nod to the dealer, who secures my chips until we decide what to play next.

"How much do you think we're up?" she asks.

"I'd say somewhere around twelve hundred."

"We're on a roll then. What should we play next?" She looks around the room. Her eyes settle on something across the room. "How good are you at blackjack?"

"I've been known to hold my own." She smiles at me.

Taking my arm, she lets me escort her to the tables. Two chairs are open next to each other. Our chips are split between us.

"Have you played?" I ask while the pit boss trades out the decks. She leans over, her lips brushing my ear.

"I've been known to count cards," she whispers. Sitting up, she winks at me. The cards are dealt as soon as our bets are placed. Geneva immediately splits her pair. Another martini is set on the table at her elbow. If my count is correct, that's martini number four.

"Play," she says, nudging me with her body. My mind refocuses on my cards.

"Hit," I bark.

It doesn't take me long to bust. Geneva, however, wins. We fall into a steady rhythm of growing one pile of chips and then the other. She can hold her own as well as any player in the room. Another hour passes before we notice.

"Shall we find something else?" I ask.

"We shall." She stands up from the table. There's a wobble in her stance this time. "Mr. Winsloe, would you care to escort a lady to the roulette table?"

"I would be honored, Miss Randolph."

With a laugh, we head to the next table.

seven

GENEVA

WHO KNEW gambling could be this fun? Not only does Peter look good enough to eat in his tux, but we're winning to boot.

The last time I was in Vegas, my dick of a boyfriend took up with a showgirl. Who does that in real life? Anyway, this is much better. I should stay here and become a professional blackjack player. That's probably just the martinis talking.

"Are you ready to call it a night?" Peter asks.

"But we're just getting warmed up." What is he thinking? The night is still young.

"We've been warmed up for hours now. It's two in the morning."

"Oh." I guess I didn't notice how late it had become. That's probably also the martinis' fault. "I guess if you think we should go." I hop off the stool at the baccarat table. I sway for a minute before Peter wraps a strong arm around my waist.

"I think we should." He tosses the dealer a chip. Our winnings will be sent to the room later.

Things are a little dizzy as we start from the room. It's fine though; I've never been affected too badly by alcohol. My metabolism burns it off quickly. I imagine it comes from years of martial arts training.

Peter leads us through the casino to the elevator. Weirdly, I think the liquor is hitting harder the farther I walk. It takes me a minute to focus enough to punch the up button. Has he always been this gorgeous? But I remember something about being naked. Doesn't matter; the elevator door is opening. He helps me inside, and we're joined by an older couple.

"Have I ever told you how much I want to bite that jaw?" I slur. "I'd bite that ass too if you'd let me." There's a snicker behind me.

"Geneva," he warns. Or is it an invitation? I can't tell anymore. "Sorry," he mumbles at whoever is behind me. I spin around so I can see them.

"He's biteable everywhere, don't you think?" I ask the lady. A hand clamps over my mouth.

"So sorry," he says. I try licking his hand, but he doesn't budge. The elevator opens, and I start forward. Peter pulls me back against him as the older couple steps out.

"Goodnight," the gentleman says. "And good luck."

Why would Peter need luck? I'm not going to say no.

"I can't believe you licked my hand," he complains when the doors close. He wipes his hand on his pants.

"You know you liked it." I point to the erection filling his tux pants. I'd touch it, but he pushes my hand away and we get into a slapping match. The door of the elevator opens, and I stumble, trying to get my dress to cooperate so I can get out. With a sigh, Peter picks me up in his arms.

"Is this the start of naked fun time?" It seems like a reasonable question. In the past, if a man carried me to a Vegas room, it ended in sex.

"Behave, Geneva." He sets me on my feet in front of a door. "Where's your key?"

Oh, right. I dig through my purse until I find the card. He waves it over the panel. Yay, now I can get this tight dress off. I'm suddenly so tired.

"Geneva, wait." Too late. My dress pools at my feet. I kick off my shoes and stagger toward the bedroom.

My bra is the next thing to go. I sling it to the floor next to the bed. Peter moans behind me. That reminds me, I haven't thanked him for taking me out. Spinning on my heel, I grab the front of his shirt. We crash together as my lips find his.

At first, his body stiffens like he's been bit. Then he relaxes into the kiss. His tongue slides against mine. The only way this could get better is if my nude breasts were pressed against his bare chest.

"No, Geneva." He steps away from me, but I wasn't done yet. My whole body tingles from that one kiss. "You're drunk. Get in bed before you do something you regret in the morning."

Jokes on him. Nothing I do with Peter will I ever regret. But I climb into bed like he wants. He pulls the blankets over me. The room is spinning. What did they put in those martinis?

"I put a trash can by the bed just in case," he says. "I'm sorry, I should have been paying better attention to how much you drank. I promised Rand I'd take care of you." The rest of his words are lost on me as I drift off to sleep.

* * *

When did a portal to hell open in my brain and allow a demon to crawl out? And why is the world so loud? I think I can hear it spinning on its axis.

I pry my eyes open, only to realize I'm not ready to be alive yet. The bed feels like lava, it's so hot. I kick the heavy comforter off. I don't remember the extra-large T-shirt I'm wearing. I pry my eyes open once again to read what's on it. Virginia Tech.

"Did I break the no-nudity rule?" I mumble. I can feel Peter watching me from across the room. Or at least, I can feel his presence in the room. It's like the air seems different when he's around.

"Yeah." His voice comes from the sunken living area.

"Have you been here long?" I ask, attempting to sit up. My head pounds. It takes a few minutes of swallowing to convince my stomach to behave.

"I ordered some lunch," he says, ignoring my question. He appears at the side of the bed. "Here." He hands a bottle of water to me. "I'll get you something for your head after you eat."

"Did you at least have fun last night?" I take a sip of the water.

"You know," he says after some consideration, "I did. We won around five grand."

"Are you serious?"

"As death and taxes."

"Where did we do the best?"

"Probably at one of the poker tables. I think everyone was too busy trying to look down your dress to pay attention. You kept bending to whisper in my ear. It was a brilliant strategy," he admits.

There's a knock at the door. Peter lets the server in with

a cart of food. It smells both amazing and disgusting at the same time.

Crawling out of bed, I pull on a pair of leggings. The T-shirt is already warm, so there's no reason to trade it out. I start down the steps into the living area when my bladder reminds me I drank a lot of vodka last night. By the time I return, Peter has everything on the table and the server is gone.

"Did you leave anything for the rest of the hotel?" I sass, sliding into one of the chairs at the small dining table.

"Don't bite the hand that's feeding you."

"But you're so very biteable," I tease back.

"Or so you told the old couple in the elevator last night."

"I did not."

"You did. I think she was scandalized. He thought it was hilarious."

"I wish I had it on video." I laugh. The look on his face must have been priceless. "Did you pop a chub?"

"Geneva," he scolds.

Have I mentioned how much I like the way my name rolls off his tongue? Why else would I taunt him so much?

His eyes suddenly narrow as they home in on me. "Why? Does the idea make you wet?"

"Shame on you, Peter Winsloe." I wave a french fry at him. "Breaking your own rules."

He rolls his eyes and shakes his head. It's an impressive act of multitasking.

"What would your mother say if she knew you talk like that?"

"My mother would beat me bloody if she heard me say that to a lady," he says.

"Good thing there're no ladies around here."

His eyebrows draw together in a scowl. "When you say things like that, it makes me want to bend you over my knee."

"Now that idea makes me wet," I say.

"How about you put that mouth to better use?" I raise an eyebrow at him. "I mean by eating."

"Eating what?" I bat my eyes at him.

"Geneva, eat." He jabs a finger at my plate. Looks like I won this round. Peter never stood a chance.

I wolf down the burger and fries he ordered me. I know: carbs, carbs, carbs. Sue me. It's been a long time since that salad yesterday. Peter shakes two ibuprofen into his hand, and I wash them down with a diet soda. I already feel better.

"What are we doing with the rest of the day?" I ask.

"What would you like to do?"

"Hmmm." I think about it for a minute. I don't think I can do another night of gambling. There's a very good chance the last one almost killed me. "You know what sounds nice? An afternoon by the pool."

"I don't have a swimsuit with me."

"Me either, but five grand will buy one hell of a swimsuit. How about if I let you pick mine out and I'll do the same for you?" He studies me the way he always does when he thinks I'm trying to put one over on him. I'm not. I just think he'd look amazing in a Bond-style suit. After all, we're still in Vegas. Except that the suit I have in mind, I'm hoping to see it more in Austin.

"Do you want me to book you a message after?" he asks.

"Only if you do one with me. They can finish working on those sore muscles."

"Fine, you get dressed. I'll make the reservations."

He moves to the phone in the living area, and I head for the bathroom and a much-needed shower. I can smell the vodka trying to leave my body. It's not a good smell. By the time I'm finished getting ready, Peter has everything booked. He even knows the best place to find swimsuits.

The shops are teeming with people when we reach them. Peter stays close to me so we don't get separated. That's what he claims anyway. It doesn't explain why that includes his hand on my lower back as we walk around. The shop that sells swimsuits is past the restaurant from last night. It looks like it has some possibilities.

"What do you think about this one?" I ask, stepping out of the dressing room. Peter decided he would simply approve or veto what I choose. The first number is a blue Brazilian bikini that fades to white on the top. He nods when I show him the front. Then I turn around. He grunts.

"No." That's all he says.

"What's wrong with it? I think it's cute."

"Your ass is in full view of any letch by the pool. It's a hard no."

"Are you one of the letches?"

"Absolutely. Next."

I laugh and return to the dressing room. Based on the way he adjusted his jeans, this one is a keeper. I'll just slip it in when he's not looking. The next one is a little more conservative. It's a tankini with a skirt. It's red with white polka dots all over it. I step out of the dressing room. He scowls.

"Well, you don't have to dress like a nun from the nineteen-twenties." He twirls his hand, and I turn around. "You look like a nightmare Minnie Mouse." I cock a hip. "You do," he insists.

With a huff, I return behind the curtain.

I hurl back the curtain with an indignant flourish this time. The current swimsuit is a simple black bikini. The only frill is the mesh at my hips holding the bottom together. My boobs are pressed into a rather impressive handful inside the full cups.

Peter is sitting with one leg crossed over the other. He looks like a Mafia don inspecting his merchandise.

"Turn," he growls, and I obey. He stands and stalks toward me. With his hand sliding over my stomach, he spins us toward the mirror. In our reflection, he stands behind me with his large hand splayed on my torso. It's possessive and demanding. My core heats as he leans forward. "It's perfect," he whispers in my ear.

He's not lying; it is perfect. Even if I didn't know that Peter was incapable of lying to me, the bulge pressing against my ass tells the story. He has a very obvious tell when it comes to my body. I first noticed it when I was in high school.

Rand and I had accepted an invitation to the Winsloes for Thanksgiving. I bent over to pull a board game off the lower shelf. When I stood back up, I found Peter staring at me. His pants had grown much tighter in that brief period. He finally cleared his throat and excused himself from the room. Since then, I've watched how certain things I do or wear affect him.

"You like it?" I ask.

"I do."

"Now we just have to find you something." I step away. "Give me a second to change back." What I don't say is just how wet this swimsuit already is. I have to buy it now.

Quickly, I change back into my street clothes. I know exactly where to find Peter's next swimsuit.

"Head into the dressing room. I'll be right there," I tell him as I brush past. They don't have the La Perla one Daniel Craig wore, but I find the next best thing. My mouth is watering just thinking about him in it.

PETER

"GENEVA, there's no way I can wear this," I say. She's lost her mind. It takes a lot of work just to get the damn swimsuit on.

"What's wrong with it?" she asks. I step out of the dressing room.

"If I move too quickly, my junk is going to fall out. It's at least two sizes too small." She's staring at me like I'm her next meal. Her eyes slowly peruse down until they stop at the tightest part. Please don't pop a chub. There's no way it'll survive in this suit.

"I think it's perfect," she says.

"Okay, first, my eyes are up here, you perv." I motion to my face. She smiles at me. "Second, no." I turn to walk back into the dressing room.

"Damn," she moans.

Easy boy, she's just trying to get a rise out of you. Literally.

"You have to let me smack it."

"Geneva," I warn, stepping through the curtain. I love saying her name. It feels like a cool breeze on a warm summer night. I say it as often as I can. "Find something else."

The next one she throws over the curtain looks a little larger, but it's gray. Who wears a gray swimsuit? I pull it on anyway and step out. Holding my arms out to the side, I do a three-sixty. She has a wicked smile on her face. She's up to something I've missed.

"What?" I ask. "Why would you choose gray?" Why would a store even carry this color? It's going to look like I'm naked in the water. You can also see every inch of my cock.

Oh. I don't even argue with her this time. I just return to the dressing room. "Try again."

"Fine," she says. I can hear the pout in her voice. It makes me smile. Maybe I'll take the gray one for later. A new suit shoots over the curtain rail at me. It's not bad. I pull it on and step back out. This suit is blue with red stripes down the legs. It has a retro-athletic feel to it that I like.

"Turn," she snarls, like I did with her last suit. That thing made her luscious breasts look amazing. Laying by the pool next to them will be the death of me. I do a slow turn while she appraises my trunks. They're still tight, but not uncomfortably so. "These are nice."

"Yeah?"

"Yeah. They hug everywhere they should but still look classic. I say yes."

"Shall we check out then?" I ask.

"We shall." She precedes me to the cashier. We pile our suits on the counter, and I notice out of the corner of my eye that she's decided to buy the Brazilian anyway. Fine by me.

Rand has a house in Austin with a private pool. I wouldn't mind seeing it make an appearance there. While he and his wife are back in Dansboro Crossing, of course.

We stroll back through the shops and head up to our rooms. Geneva decides I need to pick her up at her room in fifteen minutes to head to the pool, so I hurry into my room.

Shedding my clothes, I pull on the new suit and throw a T-shirt on to walk to the pool area. I don't have anything but tennis shoes in the room, so I pull them back on. I'm knocking on her door in exactly fifteen minutes.

"May I escort you somewhere wet?" I ask when she opens the door.

"You really can't help yourself, can you?" She steps out in one of the hotel robes.

"I can't. I might have to throw that rule out."

"Good. Now I just have three to work on." She smiles at me. I cock an eyebrow at her. You would think I'd be so over this trip already. Geneva taunts me at every turn.

Except I'm not. I love sparring with this woman. I hate to tell her she broke the nudity one also. As long as she doesn't remember (she's at least not mentioned it), then it'll be my dirty little secret.

I have kissed her before, in case you're wondering. Last night wasn't our first one. The last time I was fifteen though. We were in the basement of my house playing truth or dare with a couple of friends over the holidays. I chose dare, and my older brother, Tim, dared me to kiss her. He knew I had a crush on Geneva already. I was so nervous my palms were sweating. It wasn't very memorable.

Last night's kiss, however, was one for the record books. Even inebriated, she kissed like a rock star. With her naked breasts pressed against my chest, it was all I could do not to throw her on the bed and strip her out of those barely-there panties.

Fortunately, common sense took over. I can't strip off the barely-there panties of my best friend's sister. That's what I'm telling myself anyway. Over and over.

"Come on, the pools are heated," I say when we step outside. She shivers in the cold air. The pools may be heated, but it's still late fall. I lead her to the nearest deck chair, and she slides out of her robe and dives into the pool. I peel off my T-shirt and shoes to follow her. The water feels amazing.

"Do you remember the time you came with Rand to California for spring break? We kept getting paired up to chicken fight in the pool?" she asks.

How could I forget? I had to threaten half the neighborhood kids so I always got Geneva. She sat the entire week with her pussy pressed against the back of my neck. I was in heaven. I was also in hell knowing that was as close as I'd get to it.

"Yeah, I was what, sixteen?"

"That sounds right. I would have been fifteen. I'm surprised you didn't drown."

"If memory serves, we ruled the pool that week."

"We did." She floats closer to me. It's cold enough outside that we hunker in the water up to our necks. Suddenly, she pushes out of the water and forces me underneath the surface. I come up sputtering.

"Here's where you die, Randolph," I say.

Diving under the water, I grab her good ankle and pull her under. When I resurface, she's laughing. I don't remember a time when I've seen Geneva this relaxed. She's always had to wear a tough shell around her. First to survive her father. Then to keep the world from closing in on her. I like this carefree Geneva.

"I'll race you to the end," she says before diving. I grin before diving after her. We spend the rest of our time racing around the pool until we're both spent.

"We should head to our massages," I suggest. We climb from the pool quickly. It's colder than when we dived in. She pulls her robe around her; I towel dry. We both hurry inside to the spa.

The attendant trades us for new robes. Geneva disappears into the women's locker room. I spin-dry my suit and then shower off the chlorine. Placing the suit inside a locker, I tighten the robe around my naked body and walk into the relaxation room.

"Close your eyes," Geneva says when she joins me. She places cucumbers on my eyes. I feel her sit on the lounger next to me. "I'm looking forward to this," she whispers. Me too, but it's going to be awkward. All they had available was a couple's massage room. I guess the nudity rule is about to go out the window.

"Mr. and Mrs. Winsloe, we're ready for you," an attendant announces from the doorway. Geneva cuts her eyes at me. I shake my head in apology. I'm sure I'll hear about this later. We follow the woman to the treatment room. "I'll leave you to get comfortable on the tables." The door closes, and I turn to Geneva.

"I think I would remember getting married last night," she says.

"Sorry, this is all they had. I just booked it under my name. They must have assumed we were married. I'll turn my back so you can get on the table first."

"Why bother if we're already married?"

She slides the robe off her shoulders, and my mouth goes dry. Perfection stands in front of me in all her glory.

Best friend's sister, best friend's sister, I chant in my head.

Oh, fuck it. I slide my robe off and raise my arms partway in an aggressive gesture. She takes her time perusing my body. I've got to get on this table before I have a full-blown kickstand to fight with.

We're both lying under the sheets when the therapists enter the room. It's a man-and-woman team. The woman moves to Geneva. I'm good with that. I might have to rip the man's arms off if he touched her. I know he's a professional, but just no. They go over the rules and whip the sheets down to our waists. A moan escapes Geneva when the therapist presses up her back. This was a horrible idea.

"Oh my god, this was a brilliant idea, Peter," she moans.

"Maybe you should stay super silent to get the best experience," I suggest. The moans are going to kill me.

"Problem?" I hear her laugh.

"When you're involved, always." Geneva releases a drawn-out moan worthy of an Academy Award. "Funny."

"Are you okay?" the therapist asks.

"She's just torturing me," I say. "She obviously needs to be committed."

"Don't make me come bite those glutes," Geneva says.

"You're likely to break your teeth on these things," my therapist points out. "What have you been doing?" His knuckles press deeply into the muscles.

"Owww," I whine. The next time he presses against them, I manage just a wince. It's the one area I wouldn't let Geneva use her magical muscle balm on me. Now I regret that decision. "Jesus," I huff the next time. Who knew your ass could take such a beating climbing down a mountain trail?

At last, the torture ends. Pulling our robes back on, we

leave the spa for our rooms. We get curious looks in the elevator. Geneva doesn't comment on her obsession with biting me this time at least.

"You want to throw on pajamas and come watch a movie in my room?" I ask when we reach my door. "I'll order in."

"Sure. Give me ten minutes."

I prop the door open with the safety bar so she can let herself in. I'll put off taking a shower for a little while so the oil can soak in. My butt muscles are finally starting to loosen. I guess that's good news. Pulling on a pair of flannel sleep pants and a T-shirt, I return to the living area just in time to see Geneva step through the door.

"What do you want to eat?" I ask, picking up the phone.

"Salad."

"Yes, I'll take a Cobb with the dressing on the side. I'll also order the filet cooked medium rare, fries, and two Negra Modelos." I raise an eyebrow in question at her. She nods her consent. This isn't our first rodeo. I know exactly what salad is her favorite, that she's going to steal half my fries, and that she likes dark beer.

I don't remember exactly when Geneva and I started hanging out together as friends. It crept up on us slowly. I do know that since Rand moved, she's been a fixture in my apartment most nights. Often, she swung by after martial arts practice. She'd shower while I cooked. We'd eat and find a movie we could both tolerate.

"Any movie requests"" she asks. She flops down on one end of the couch, and I join her.

"Surprise me."

"You know I'll make you sit through cheesy B-rated rom-com if you say that just to be mean."

"Fine. Psychological thriller."

"Ooh, good choice." She flips through the online movies until she settles on something we haven't seen yet. She curls up against me, and I throw a blanket over our legs to keep us warm.

I know we look like an old married couple already. Except, I can't keep Geneva the way I want to. A romantic breakup would destroy this. I'm living in a quandary. I don't want to give her up, but I can't keep her either. Life isn't fair.

nine

GENEVA

I FEEL MUCH BETTER this morning when I wake up. Except that this is a really small bed, and I'm on fire. One eye pries open, then the other. I'm not in bed. I obviously fell asleep watching movie number three. I'm also not on fire, there's simply a burly, warm body wrapped around me. Peter snores softly behind me.

"Peter," I say, nudging him. He's pressed up against my back. His impressive morning wood is tucked between my ass cheeks. Normally, I'd be good with that, except I really need the bathroom. "Pete."

"What?" he growls in my ear.

"Let me up. We fell asleep on the couch." I try to unwrap his arms from my body. The harder I try, the tighter he holds on. "Peter!"

"Fine," he grumbles. I kick the blanket off me and stand up. He snatches it back under his chin.

Something you might not know about Peter Winsloe is that he's a snuggler. It's why Rand would rather sleep on the floor than have to share a bed with him. There have been times when they traveled in the past when that was their only option. Personally, I kind of like the snuggling.

When I return from the bathroom, he's still sprawled on the couch. I take one of the chairs next to it rather than wrestle him for the space. He slings the blanket at me and sits up.

"Want some breakfast?" I ask.

"Yeah. Surprise me." He scratches the side of his face where his beard was. Standing, he takes a minute to find his balance. It gives me time to admire the impressive tent in the front of his pajama pants. I've seen it a few times over the years. It never fails to make my mouth water.

"Stop staring, or it won't go down," he grouches and moves toward the bathroom.

"I don't mind so much if it doesn't go down," I call after him. He grunts, then the bathroom door closes.

I pick up the phone and order a western omelet for Peter. The spinach frittata with goat cheese works for me. I also order two large glasses of orange juice. I figure we could both use the vitamin C before continuing on today.

He flops back down on the couch. Sadly, the tent is no longer pitched.

"Sorry. I don't remember falling asleep," he says. "We'll eat and then head out."

The food arrives. We discuss the day while we eat. Afterward, I return to my room to pack. The formal clothes were returned yesterday while I was sleeping half the day away. It doesn't take long to gather the rest of my things up.

There's a knock on the door, and I let Peter in. It's fine for him to prop the door open, but if I do it, I get a lecture.

"Got everything?" He takes my bag out of my hand. We check out and retrieve the Rover from the valet. Part of me is sad to see Vegas go. The other part can't wait to ride horses in Zion National Park.

Peter told me over breakfast that he booked us into a bed-and-breakfast near the park for tonight. From what he described, it sounds quaint. As long as there's a soaker tub, I don't care.

"Ready?" he asks as I climb into the SUV. "I think it's around five hours or so."

"Lead on. I'll get the next quiz ready," I tease.

He groans.

"This one is titled: Will he be great in bed?"

"How many quizzes are in that magazine?"

"Question one," I say, ignoring him. "Do you trust him?" I study Peter until he raises an eyebrow at me. We roll slowly out of Las Vegas. "Totally. Top marks for trustworthiness."

"That's good to know, I guess. It's a little late if not; I already have you trapped in a car with me."

"What's the first thing you notice when you walk into his bedroom?" That one takes me a moment. "Have I ever been in your bedroom?"

"You slept in my bedroom at my parents' house," he points out.

"Yeah, but that was your childhood bedroom. It smelled like Axe body spray and teenage frustration." He laughs, which makes me smile. "I don't think I've ever snooped around your adult bedroom. Stop. Go back and set it back up so I can see what it smells like."

"It smells very nice, trust me. I've moved on to Polo."

"Hmmm. I'll just have to take your word for it. Remind me to smell your bedroom when we get to Austin."

"Noted."

"Oooh, is he a good dancer? Do you dance other than stiffly at formal functions?"

"I've been known to cut a rug," he answers. "I'm not stiff either."

"Not right now, anyway." I make a point to look at his crotch. "Square dancing then." He smirks. "So a firm no. Shame, I can twerk like no one's business." I peer back down at the magazine. "Is he patient and confident? Like a saint."

"Not always."

"How do you know I'm talking about you?"

"I guess I don't."

"I am by the way. You are the most patient man in the world," I say. "I'm thinking about hosting a roast for your next birthday."

He sighs loudly.

"Moving on. When he talks to you, does he hold eye contact?" I stare at him. He looks over at me. "How else would I have become so obsessed with those Caribbean eyes?" His smile is shy this time. "Speaking of, what color eyes do you think I have? No one ever gets this one right."

"Green," he says without hesitation. "With just a touch of gold in them. They remind me of jade when you're tired. They're almost emerald when you're up to something. When you're angry, they look like a storm brewing in the Atlantic Ocean."

My mouth hangs open. Most men can't even tell me if they're light or dark. Peter knows more about me than anyone I've been in a relationship with. It's hard to express how being that seen makes me feel.

It would be so easy to fall in love with him. He's made it very clear, however, that can never happen. I close my eyes to regain my balance. When I open them, he's watching me out of the corner of his eye.

"Does he interrupt you?" I say, pressing on. "Only when I embarrassed him."

"You never embarrass me," he argues. "I just don't want anyone to get the wrong idea about us."

"Heaven forbid." I roll my eyes. "Is he a good kisser? I don't think I can judge based on that one game in the basement of your house." He smiles like he has a secret. "What?"

"Nothing. Go on."

"No, you know something I don't. What is it?" I cross my arms and wait for him to spill.

"You don't remember kissing me the night before last?" he asks.

"No." I'm shocked again. I don't remember that at all. Damn it. "When did I kiss you?"

"You were drunk. It didn't mean anything."

"Was it at least good?" I'm going to be pissed however he answers. If it was good, I totally missed out. If it wasn't, well, I don't know, but that's not nice to admit.

"Very good." He grins.

"I'm going to mark that as an affirmative then. But we're going to have to circle back around to that one."

He shakes his head, but I see a smile in the corners of his mouth.

"Last question. Does he make you feel sexy?" My mind reels back to all of the times I've caught Peter looking at me. The way he growled in the dressing room when I flashed my bare ass at him. How his eyes devoured me in the spa room when I dropped the robe. How I wanted more every time. I guess I've been silent too long.

"If it helps," he says, "you are the sexiest woman I

know. Your brother would kill me for saying that, but it's the truth. You light up every room you walk into. Every man in the high roller's room wanted you. If they knew you the way I do, I wouldn't have been able to beat them off."

"How do you know me?" I whisper.

"I know what's inside. That you're brilliant. You're braver than you should have to be. You are fucking fierce. That you might bust balls, but you can't see a stray animal without taking care of it. I know you volunteer at the children's shelter because you don't want even one more child to feel alone like you did growing up."

"Stop, Peter," I beg. I swipe at a tear threatening to roll down my cheek.

"I know you're beautiful inside and out," he finishes. "I don't need some quiz to tell me that."

I think this is the moment I give up trying to not fall in love with Peter Winsloe. It's hopeless when he sees me the way he does. I don't deserve someone like him. He's light where I'm trapped in darkness.

I want so desperately to be who he thinks I am. I might help animals and children, but I also took up a martial art that leaves me bloody for a reason. I watched my brother take my beatings for so long that it did something to me. I'm not whole inside.

I toss the magazine in the back seat and stare out the window. It's impossible for me to ever live up to what Peter sees. I steel myself against the heartache of knowing that.

I'll show him I'm not worth his time. He'll learn I'm nothing more than something to do in passing. I'll never be the small-town, picket fence kind of woman. I'm good for a quick fuck, then move along. I take a deep breath. The sooner Peter learns that, the better we'll both be.

"I'm not sorry I said it," he begins.

"Are we stopping to eat anytime in the near future?" I snap back.

"Yeah. We're coming into a small town. Hopefully, they have something worth eating." His voice sounds resigned. Good.

The diner we pull into is even smaller than the last one. It has tired-looking curtains hanging on the windows. The seats are in need of repair. We're led to a booth in the corner. A paper sign says the special is spicy pork tamales. Whatever. We both order the special and sodas. Peter watches me closely as I stare out into the diner.

"How did I piss you off this time?" he asks. "Does the truth make you angry? Do you want me to see you how your father does? As a waste of DNA? Something to be cast aside, not even worth striking? Because I'll never see you as less than special."

"Peter," I say with a sigh. "You don't know me. Not really."

"I know exactly who you are."

I'm saved from continuing this pointless conversation by the waitress delivering our meal. There's no use trying to change his mind. He'll learn on his own soon enough. When we get to Austin and he figures out I'm not good at anything but putting together ads. I can't help run a business.

"This isn't half bad," he continues. He's giving me a reprieve for now. I'm sure we'll revisit this later. "It's not much to look at, but it's edible."

I take a bite. He's right; it's much better than it looks. I'm not embarrassed to admit that I clean my plate. The frittata had worn off long ago. My soda came from a machine also. This is fresh and still has a bite to it. When we get back to the car, I'm leaving a hell of a review.

Peter smiles at me. It's a truce offering. I meet it with a smile of my own. We never could stay irritated with each other.

We pass the rest of the drive listening to music in companionable silence. I can't believe the small cabin we finally pull up in front of. It's even more quaint than the one in Yosemite. Peter fishes our bags out of the back. I meet him on the front porch, and he punches in a code for the door.

"Is that a goat?" I ask before we can step inside.

"Appears to be. There's also a couple of donkeys over there."

"How rustic are these cabins?" I'm actually itching to go pet a donkey. I don't want to admit it to him though. I'll never hear the end of it.

"There's a soaker tub. You're good." He steps inside the cabin. It's not bad. Old but comfortable. "Want to go pet the donkeys before we settle in for the evening? I'm making dinner tonight."

"How do you always read my mind?" I ask. I grab his hand and pull him back outside toward the donkey enclosure. Fuck it. He can tease all he wants. I love tiny donkeys.

"I told you, I know what's in your heart better than you do."

He might, and it scares me. Can he see how black it is? I sigh. It doesn't matter right now. I have donkeys to pet. Maybe goats too.

ten

PETER

THERE'S NOT much time to enjoy the cabin or the donkeys, for that matter. I made dinner for us, and we turned in early. Everything is packed back into the Rover early the next morning. Geneva loves horses, so I booked us an overnight ride through most of Zion. We have to meet our outfitter at the trailhead at sunup.

Geneva grew up riding horses. It's what all of the private school girls did, apparently. I can ride well enough to fake it through the test. I thought it made sense to insist we lead ourselves through the park. Now, I'm rethinking that decision.

"Do you have everything?" our wrangler asks. He's meeting us at the other end. I paid extra to have our campsite set up. After a day of riding, I didn't want to have to pitch a tent, cook dinner, and help with the horses.

"Looks like you've thought of everything," I say. "Wait, Geneva. Let me help you." She's still nursing her sore ankle. I cup my hands and lift her onto her horse.

Her horse is named Eros, after the Greek god of love and desire. It's a beautiful red sorrel with a flowing mane. As if it knows it's beautiful, it prances around ready to hit the trail.

"We'll see you on the other side." The wrangler waves and returns to his truck.

I swing up into the saddle. My horse is named Cupcake, I guess after the delicious tiny dessert. He's large and stout, much like me. He doesn't prance. As a matter of fact, he barely moves.

"Looks like we head this direction," Geneva says, checking the map. Also, there's a sign that points us in the correct direction, but I won't point that out. I let her lead the way. The smile on her face is worth the beating my legs and ass are about to take. It doesn't take long to realize riding is better than hiking though.

The views are stunning. The park is rough and rugged, unlike anything I'm used to. We see very few other people passing this way. It helps that fall has set in. The temperature is cold enough to require several layers.

"This is amazing," Geneva says over her shoulder. "I'm so glad we're doing this. To think you wanted to just fly to Austin." She smiles before turning back around.

"Yeah, what was I thinking?" I laugh.

It seems like we've been riding for hours when she pulls her horse to a stop.

"Ready for lunch?" she asks. I stop her before she can swing off of her horse. "I can get it, you know."

"I know," I say, sliding to the ground. "But let's not take a chance on tearing up that ankle again." I help ease her to the ground.

We tie our horses to some sturdy-looking scrub plants. She pulls sandwiches from her saddlebags while I unhook our canteens. We sit on the side of the trail with our legs out to take in the view as we eat.

"Is it weird that a sack lunch always tastes better outdoors?" she asks.

"We used to eat lunch in the tree house Dad built all summer when we were growing up," I say. "We built a hoist with a basket to haul it up. Mom would load it every day at noon with enough to feed an army."

"That sounds nice."

"It was." We eat for a few minutes in silence. "It's still there. The tree house."

"I remember it. It looked amazing. I guess we were too old to still climb trees when I came to your house."

"We should build Keats one. Rand can send sandwiches up in the summers."

She smiles and rises to her feet. Taking my trash, she stuffs it back in her saddlebag. I help her back on her horse. She turns her horse toward the trail, and I have to scramble to catch up.

She's upset about something. Is it the tree house? I know she never had one. Her father would never have spent time helping her build something so frivolous.

"I'll build you a tree house too," I say. "I can send you lunch up in a lift all summer. It'll be your remote office."

I hear her chuckle. I like that sound. She reins in her horse and turns to face me.

"I don't need a tree house," she says.

"What do you need?"

"I don't know yet," she says. For a minute, she stares at the scenery. "You'll be the first to find out though when I figure it out." She gives me a salute and continues down the trail.

I now have the rest of the day to guess what she needs. I

shouldn't be the man who gives it to her, but I'm desperate to anyway.

I'm contemplating that question when I see her horse go down in front of me. My heart leaps into my throat. Geneva goes over its shoulder and lands on the ground.

I'm off my horse faster than I thought possible. Eros hops back up to his feet. Peels of laughter ring from Geneva. When I reach her, she's sitting on the ground, still holding the reins.

"What happened?" I ask, sliding to my knees in front of her.

"I'm not sure. One moment I'm taking in the scenery from the back of Eros; the next minute I'm sitting here."

"Are you hurt?"

"I don't think so." I search her legs, check on her ankle, and help her to her feet. "Something is wrong with Eros though." Her hand runs down the horse's leg. It picks its hoof up when she reaches the fetlock. "The shoe isn't loose." Her fingers probe the hoof until she finds a sore spot on the frog. "I think he has a stone bruise."

"We're going to have to lead him the rest of the way," I state. "You can ride with me." She looks at me, then around me to Cupcake. I'm not sure if she's questioning the horse being able to hold both of our weights. I should probably be insulted. "Or you can take Cupcake and I'll lead Eros out," I grumble. A smile lights up her face.

"Do you want to drive or ride shotgun?" she asks.

"Your choice."

"I'll drive. At least for a while." She ties one of Eros's reins to his saddle and takes the other in her hand. We transfer the gear from my horse to hers. I help her on Cupcake, then swing up behind her.

There's no way we both fit on the saddle. I'm relegated

to the space on his rump behind it. It's going to be a long ride with no padding or stirrups. "Ready?"

"Drive on," I say. She hands me Eros's remaining rein to hold. I snake a hand around her waist. I sure don't want to fall off from back here. It takes a moment to convince the horse to follow us. I quickly become an expert in pulling along a pack animal behind us.

We continue down the Wildcat Canyon trail to the connector and into the Hop Valley. Eros limps behind us the entire way. I'm positive that I have no feeling in my ass. This time, if she wants to rub all over it with her balm, I might just let her.

The Hop Valley turns out to be the best part of the ride. It switches back through one of the creeks several times.

The first creek crossing, I thought I was going in when Eros hesitated on the bank. With a little coaxing, he finally followed. Poor guy has to be exhausted. There's no way, though, we could leave him behind. The wranglers will be waiting for us at camp. He'll be well attended to then.

"Would you like to trade?" Geneva asks, pulling Cupcake to a stop.

"I'm fine. I don't think if I get off, I'll ever make it back on."

"You must be dying."

"I can think of worse ways to spend the day," I answer. "Getting to spoon you the whole way is a definite bonus." I squeeze my arm to pull her closer.

"One of these days we should reverse so I get to be the big spoon." She encourages Cupcake to continue down the trail.

"Do we, though?"

"It seems reasonable. You shouldn't be the only one who gets to hoard all the big spoon power."

"Geneva," I scold. "You always have all the power, whether you're the big spoon or not." She leans back against my chest and kisses my cheek. "What was that for?" I'm not complaining. I need more information so I can make it happen again.

"For being you, Peter Winsloe. You don't need a super-power, you are a superpower."

"I think that's the nicest thing you've ever said to me." I blush, but, fortunately, no one can see it except Eros. I don't think he'll rat me out.

"Then that's my fault. You deserve to hear nice things." I don't know what's happened to her. Maybe all the bouncing on Cupcake has done something to her brain. We've never said nice things to each other. Snark is our thing.

"Don't go all soft on me, ice princess."

"Fuck you, Winsloe," she snarls.

"That's better." I kiss her on the temple. We ride the rest of the way in silence, but she's not pissed at me, though. The smile on her face every time we splash into the creek tells me everything.

* * *

GENEVA

I don't think I've ever heard a moan so heartfelt as the one that just came out of Peter at the sight of camp ahead of us. In my defense, I did offer to trade with him.

The wranglers are waiting for us at a large tent. There's a fire made in a fire pit and chairs set up for us. Peter has thought of everything. I can't wait to spend a night under the stars. Or in a tent under the stars.

"What happened?" Rusty, our red-haired wrangler, asks. He meets us a short distance from the camp.

"I think it's a stone bruise." I swing my leg over to hop down when a strong arm tightens around me. Slowly, Peter lowers me to the ground. "He fell on the West Rim trail. He's got a skinned knee too."

"Hey buddy." Rusty examines the hoof, coming to the same conclusion. "I'm sorry about this."

"I'm just sorry he got hurt."

"We'll take them back and bring fresh horses tomorrow morning," he assures me. "Do you need help getting down?" he calls to Peter. Peter is laid over on the saddle with his forehead resting on the horn.

"Come on, big man," I say. "Let's give those balls a rest."

He slings his leg over Cupcake's rump and slides down. I keep my hand on his back the whole way. The look on his face when his feet meet the ground speaks volumes. I'm not sure his ass will ever be the same. He hands Cupcake's reins to Rusty.

"We'll see you first thing in the morning," Rusty says.

Peter just grunts. He walks to the fire to check on the pot hanging over it.

"That's chili. The fixings are in the cooler when you're ready to eat." The wrangler loads the horses in a stock trailer and pulls out of camp. We're alone once again.

"Are you going to survive?" I ask.

"Yeah, I'm good," Peter answers. He's not good, he just doesn't want to spoil the adventure for me. "Hungry?"

"I could eat." We set about pulling everything we need out of the coolers. "I've never had Frito pie," I announce, pulling a bag of corn chips out.

"I thought you should before we get to Austin. It's a

staple in the south." He stirs the chili to make sure it's not scorching on the bottom.

"What do I do?" I've pulled out an enamel bowl that looks like something from the pictures of cattle drives.

"Start with chips." I pile chips in my bowl. He takes it and spoons a helping of chili over the chips. "Now add whatever else you want. Looks like we have onions, cheese, and jalapeños."

"I'll do it all." He watches me pile peppers on top before picking up his bowl. I take a seat by the fire. He joins me shortly with a small towel. "These bowls do heat up." I set the bowl on the towel.

Tentatively, I take my first bite. Flavors explode in my mouth. It's hot, both from the heat and spicy. There's salty from the chips, creamy from the cheese, and just the perfect blend of spices in the chili.

"If this is what they eat in Austin all the time, I'm on board," I say around a mouthful.

"I don't think they eat this all the time," he says. "Remember all the barbecue and Tex-Mex we ate when hunting for office space?"

"You won't miss Nor-Cal food?"

"I'm sure they have plenty of sushi places too. You can still eat your raw fish."

I laugh. Tonight is perfect. Even if Peter still looks like he sat on a thorn bush, he's here beside me. The sky is full of stars as far as I can see. The food is good, and the banter is even better. Did I mention there's only one tent?

eleven

PETER

I LOVE WATCHING Geneva when her walls are down. It's worth every sore muscle to see her smile like that.

I took a chance on the Frito pies as she's a strictly healthy eater. Nothing usually passes her lips that isn't analyzed to death for its calorie count, carbohydrates, or protein content. Let's face it, there's nothing healthy about corn chips covered in chili.

"I've got the stuff for s'mores too," I mention.

"Peter Winsloe," she says with a cute little gasp. "Now I know you're trying to seduce me. My panties are going to melt right off with all of that dirty talk."

I grin. I can't help it. What do you do with a woman this sassy? Never have I had anyone else tell me I'll melt their panties off. Especially not just by offering toasted marshmallows and chocolate.

"In that case, let me get the marshmallows," I tease back. I stand and take the bowl from her hands. Rusty left a sealed box to put the dirty dishes in. No washing for me. I love camping like this. Is this what they call glamping?

Pulling the s'mores ingredients from another box, I slide a marshmallow on one of the roasting sticks.

"Here." I hand her the stick, and she holds it over the fire.

By the time she has her marshmallow toasted, I've assembled the rest of her s'more. She places the gooey mess on the graham cracker so I can squish it off the stick. She takes a bite of the concoction. I swear her eyes roll into the back of her head.

"Oh my god," she croons, and my cock naturally stirs in my pants. At least it's reliable. "What genius came up with these?"

"I think some Girl Scout leader."

"Damn, I missed out on being one of those. All those cute uniforms. S'mores. Badges." She winks at me.

"Yeah, I was pretty sexy in khaki," I say. She grins. "You know Rand was in scouts also."

"What?" She looks like I could knock her over with a marshmallow, she's so in shock.

"Yep. He joined after we met at school. I was already in a troop when I transferred. He wanted to learn the outdoor skills I kept bragging about. Where do you think he learned to sail?"

"I had no idea. Why didn't he mention it to me?"

"Do you really think Joseph Randolph would have suffered his son being a part of something he didn't handpick?"

"No, I suppose not," she admits. She's silent for a few minutes. "What else have you been keeping from me? Did we have sex in Vegas and you're just not telling me?"

"No, nothing like that happened," I answer. I smile,

trying to avoid explaining the topless kiss. She cocks an eyebrow at me. "Fine, you kissed me topless." I'm a weak man when it comes to her. It doesn't take much to pry my secrets out.

"Hmm." She stares at the fire for a few more minutes. "Did my tits look good at least?"

"They looked amazing." What? I'm not going to lie.

"I guess that's something at least." She smirks. "I'm sorry I missed it."

I shrug and slide another marshmallow on her stick. She holds it over the fire. When it's ready, I help her assemble her s'more again. She takes a bite and chews slowly. I can almost hear her mind spinning. What is she about to say this time?

Before I know what's happening, she grabs the front of my shirt. She only hesitates a second before pulling me against her. Our lips meet, and I'm kissing my best friend's sister. Again. This time with more than just my shirt between us. It barely lasts long enough for my mind to process it before she's pushed me back in my chair.

"What the hell was that?" I ask.

"I'm pissed I missed our first grown-up kiss. I was curious if it was as good as I always imagined." She's imagined kissing me?

"Well, that hardly qualifies. I wasn't ready."

"What would you do differently? Because that was just okay."

"Give me that." I snatch the remaining s'more out of her hand and toss it on the ground. Pulling her from her chair, I slide my hands through her hair. Then my lips are pressed to hers again. This time, though, I'm prepared. My tongue traces where her lips meet and she opens with a gasp. I slide inside to explore every inch.

She tastes like chocolate and corn chips. It's the best combination I've ever had.

This is nothing like the fumbled kiss in our teens. It's not even like the topless one in Vegas. This is slow and deep. It reaches from the soles of my feet to the tips of my hair. Without a doubt, I was put on this earth to kiss Geneva. How will I survive after this? There's no way I can go back to life the way it was.

"Wow," she whispers, pulling back. "You definitely get high marks."

"Geneva," I beg. I don't know if I'm begging for more or for her to force me away.

"I'm—" she begins and clears her throat. "I'm just going to get ready for bed." She stumbles toward the tent.

"Jesus," I mumble, dropping back into my chair. Now, what in the hell do I do? I won't get past a kiss like that.

Geneva obviously doesn't want anything to do with it or she wouldn't have scurried into the tent for the night. I guess I could sleep out here so it's not awkward. Although awkward seems like the one word that has defined this trip from the beginning.

I push myself out of the chair. The camp still needs to be secured for the night. It doesn't take me long to clean up, pack everything away, and put the campfire out.

Now to enter the tent. Geneva is curled up on the far cot. She's pulled the sleeping bag up to her hairline. I can't tell if she's fake sleeping so she doesn't have to talk to me or not.

Folding my clothes neatly, I lay them next to my cot. I slide into my sleeping bag in my boxer briefs. We can decide what to do about tonight sometime tomorrow.

I'm exhausted, and tomorrow is already shaping up to be another long day. Hopefully one with no unplanned injuries. I'd settle for another toe-curling kiss, though. With a last look at Geneva's back underneath her sleeping bag, I turn to the wall and drift off.

* * *

I wake the next morning to the soft tinkling of laughter from outside. The laugh I would recognize anywhere. The male voice that answers it, however, is not as familiar.

I bolt out of bed. Every muscle screams in protest. I ignore the pain as I jerk on my pants. Stomping out from behind the tent flap, I find Geneva standing at a fresh campfire. Rusty is helping her stir something.

"Good morning," she calls.

I spear Rusty with a glare. He takes a step away from her.

"Rusty is helping me learn to make gravy for our biscuits." Rusty had better back the fuck off before I render *him* into gravy. "Get dressed, it's almost ready." I reluctantly step back inside the tent. I layer back up before leaving the tent again.

"We have fresh horses," Geneva singsongs as she ladles passable-looking gravy over two dishes of biscuits. "Meet Bocephus," she says, pointing at a bay.

"He's named after Hank, Jr.," Rusty says.

"You'll be riding Widow Maker." She smirks.

"Widow Maker was Pecos Bill's horse," Rusty adds.

"Why would I want to ride a horse named that?" This doesn't bode well.

"We just call him Willie."

I don't know what to say to that. How does a horse go from a killer of men to Willie? I just grunt. It seems safer to eat rather than continue questioning the animal that has to haul my ass out of here. I fork a dripping bite of biscuit into my mouth. It's not half bad.

"See, I told you I can cook," Geneva says. She's smiling at me.

"Nice job." I nod. This is the only thing I've eaten that she's made that didn't try to poison me. She looks so proud, though, that I finish every bite on my plate. Rusty takes my empty plate to add to the stuff he's packing up.

"Today's ride isn't that far," he says. "I'll pack this up and see you there."

I leave the campfire to meet Geneva at the horses. She's as anxious to get on the trail as she was yesterday. Why do I feel like I'm dying and she appears no worse for wear? I cup my hands to help her on the horse.

Taking Willie (I refuse to call him that other name), I swing into the saddle. There are two bones in my ass I didn't know I possessed until this moment. If I just stand in the stirrups all day, I should be okay.

"Sore?" she asks me.

"How are you not?"

"I just fake it better than you," she says with a laugh. Turning her horse, we start down the trail. "Your face always tells me everything I need to know. Right now, it's begging for me to kill you and put you out of your misery. I guess my question is this: Why did you agree to the ride if you don't enjoy it?"

"Because I knew it was something you'd want to do."

"That's stupid. We could have picked something you wanted to do too."

"I don't hate this," I answer. "I'm just not in horse-riding shape. Besides, I got to spend two days with you uninterrupted by the outside world. That's worth all the pain my ass has gone through."

"Damn it, Peter. When you say things like that, I want to kiss you all over again."

"I won't say no to that." I can't stop grinning. We're having "that" conversation, and it's not as painful as I thought it would be. I like that she doesn't seem to regret kissing me. There's no doubt I'd like to continue.

"What are we going to do about this?" she asks, reining her horse to stop so she can face me.

"I don't know," I admit. "There's too much at stake. We'd still have to work together if it's short-lived. A breakup would hurt us all."

"But what if we don't break up? What if we stay together and build something amazing? Don't we owe it to ourselves to find out?" She stares at me for a beat before pushing her horse back down the trail.

She's some distance away when I finally follow. Have I been thinking about all of this wrong? Have I been so focused on an ending that I didn't even consider a future together?

We travel down the trail without speaking. My mind is too jumbled to contemplate intelligent conversation. Geneva doesn't act very inclined to talk anyway.

I think about us together. A house, kids, a thriving business? Could we really find that kind of happiness together? Do I need to just tell her brother to fuck off and go for it?

It's an easy morning ride to the trailhead. Good to his word, Rusty and his brother are there to meet us. It figures that my ass is finally acclimating to that saddle. Maybe when we get settled in Austin, we can ride more. I can't believe I'm even considering that.

I swing off of Willie, and Geneva waits this time for me to get her. We hand the reins to Rusty.

"How was it?" he asks.

"Beautiful," Geneva answers. "This has been wonderful. Thank you."

"Our pleasure, ma'am." Is Rusty flirting? I'll murder him. They'll never find his body. "Rhett is going to take you back to your car," he adds. "Thank you for your business." He holds his hand out for me to shake. Then he hugs Geneva. A growl bubbles up in my chest. Great. One real kiss, and I'm turning into a possessive alpha male asshole.

"If you'll follow me, I'll get you on the road again," Rhett pipes up. He leads us to an SUV. Geneva is offered the front passenger seat. That relegates me to the back. That's fine, I have a feeling I need to keep an eye on this wrangler-turned-Romeo also. I shouldn't have worried. Geneva falls asleep in the seat from the moment we hit the pavement.

"Thanks," I say, shaking his hand when we reach my car. I pull a sleepy Geneva out of the front seat of his SUV.

"Anytime, man." With a wave, he's gone.

"How far until we stop again?" she asks.

"Not far. You'll have just enough time to finish your nap." I settle her in the passenger seat. When I slide into the driver's side, she lays her head on my lap. My hands brush her hair behind her ear. Do I have what it takes to make this my life? House, kids, and a business?

I start the SUV and pull out of the parking lot. Maybe the Grand Canyon will hold all of the answers. I guess we'll find out.

twelve

PETER

WITH THE SEASON ENDING, I was lucky to find a rafting trip down the Colorado River at all. The guy who booked the trip warned me to bring cold water gear.

There would be a full raft of people if this were summer. He assured me there would only be a small handful this trip. We have a night to recover between high-adventure activities. Did I mention it's a two-day float trip? At least I get to sit on rubber this time.

"Wow, Peter," Geneva says, sitting up straighter in the passenger seat. I agree with her. I did a pretty good job of booking our lodgings this time. We pull under the porte cochere of an upscale-looking lodge in the South Rim of the Grand Canyon. If she thinks this is good, wait until she sees the view from our two-bedroom suite.

"We'll check in, clean up, and go find something to eat," I suggest. I know I could use a shower at this point. I drop her at the door and go to find a parking space, and I meet her at the check-in desk with our bags. A bellman takes us to our room.

"Oh my stars," she sighs when he opens the door. Directly across is a large bay window with the curtains drawn back. It offers a breathtaking view of the canyon, lit with all the glory the sinking sun has to offer. "It's beautiful." She gawks at the show outside while I deal with the bellman.

"I'm going to take a shower. I stink," I say.

"I'll go in a second." She waves me off. Her eyes haven't moved from the view.

Hot water sluicing over my body does wonders to wake me back up. The drive was beautiful but silent. Geneva didn't stir until we were already in the park. I stand in the middle of the walk-in shower as the rainhead guarantees every particle of dirt is washed down the drain.

By the time I climb out, the bathroom is steamed up. I wipe the mirror clear with my towel and study my face. The beard that's started growing back out can wait until we return from the raft trip.

"Sorry it took so long," Geneva says a little later after her shower. I'm dressed and sitting on the couch in the living area. "It was hard to convince myself to leave that rainhead." She walks across the room to look out the dark window.

"You look incredible." She does. She's wearing a pair of jeans, a long-sleeved button-down, and boots.

"You think so? It's the only southwestern outfit I own." She turns to face me. There's a smile on her face. Smiling seems to come a little easier to her now. I like to think this adventure has something to do with that. That I have something to do with that.

"I do. You look like one of the locals." Her long hair is

brushed out straight. It lies in a dark curtain down her back. My hands itch to run through it. "Ready to eat?" I say instead.

"Yes, I'm famished."

"Then we'd better go." I stand and hold open the door. "After you." She precedes me out.

The diner is mostly empty as we're shown to our seats. The menu boasts everything from steak to vegan options. I order a ribeye. Geneva decides on fish. We forgo the wine list for water. I have a feeling we'll need it over the next couple of days.

"So we'll be camping along the river tomorrow night?" she asks. I've been reviewing what the guide said on the phone. "Do we take our gear?"

"Yes, we have to do it all this time. I've got our tent and sleeping bags packed. We also need to take a change of clothes in a dry bag."

"This is why you asked me to bring my winter sailing gear?"

"It should keep you dry and reasonably warm. It's the end of the season. We're the last run before they pull out for winter. It's going to be cold on the river," I add.

"I've never done anything like this," she says. "I've ridden horses before, obviously, and I've hiked. I've even heli-skiied but never whitewater rafted."

"It should be a real learning experience for both of us."

"I can't wait," she says. Her smile makes my heart pound in my chest. Her excitement is contagious. I find myself looking forward to hurling through the freezing rapids.

"Can I ask you something?" I ask after the waitress removes our plates and serves coffee. "You said something that's had me thinking all day."

"That sounds ominous," she says.

"You said what if we don't break up, what if we stay together? Do you believe that?"

She opens her mouth. I'm sure there's something glib on her tongue. But then she reconsiders and takes a sip of coffee.

"I don't know, Peter. Maybe we stay together. Maybe it's just the thrill of the trip and we realize once we get to Austin that we're better as friends. Maybe we don't work at all, so it's something we need to get out of our systems," she says. "I just know that we've been circling each other since Rand left. It seems reasonable to see where it leads."

I focus back on the coffee in front of me. We've been circling each other longer than that. Can I press forward knowing she might not want more than one night with me? I honestly don't know where to go from here. A one-night stand has never been a problem for me. But I've never had one that involved Geneva.

"Mmm," I hum. I'll have to think about this.

"I'm sorry. I know that's not what you were looking for."

"No, it's fine," I assure her. "At least you're honest with me."

"Can I ask *you* something?" she asks.

"Of course."

"Will you promise me that, in the end, whatever happens, you won't leave? That you'll stay in Austin. That we can still be friends."

I take her hand and kiss her knuckles.

"I promise." I just hope it's a promise I can keep.

* * *

The next morning is an early one. Geneva and I both retired to our bedrooms right after dinner. The van is picking us up before daybreak, so we both needed the sleep.

We head down early for a full breakfast before moving outside with our gear. I'm worried that Geneva will be cold on the river. She assures me again she won't.

"You guys ready to raft?" a guy who looks too young to drive asks.

"We are," she answers.

He helps load her gear into the back of a van, and I'm left to heave my own crap. She's already chatting with him when I slide inside. He's explaining exactly what levels the rapids are at. I'd rather just be surprised.

There are only four other guests at the raft when we arrive. There's an older couple that I question can hold their own with a paddle. Then there's a mother and young son who look terrified. I also question their rafting abilities.

Van guy takes off after unloading our gear, and we're left with two men that look a lot more experienced. I breathe a sigh of relief. They review the safety rules, check that we have everything, and make sure that we're still comfortable going.

Climbing in the raft, Geneva takes the spot in front of me. My mind settles a little. I'll be able to keep an eye on her there. It doesn't matter if we're together or not, I'll never stop protecting her.

"Okay, folks. We're going to test your skills on one of the smaller rapids first. Ready?" Chuck, one of our guides, says and everyone cheers. Geneva leans back against me and shimmies. I guess that's her way of showing how excited she is.

Then we're being hurled through our first rapids. I paddle exactly as instructed.

"Whooo!" Geneva shouts when we are shot into calmer water.

"Yeah!" Chuck agrees. "Get ready for the next one."

That's how our morning progresses. The rapids grow steadily harder as we paddle like mad. Geneva cheers after each one. The rest of the guests join her every time. Hell, so do I after a while. It feels good to make it and still be living.

When the water calms again, the guides paddle over to the shore. We climb out while they produce lunch from one of the coolers.

"Are you enjoying it?" she asks, plopping onto the ground beside me.

"I am. Are you?"

"This has been amazing. I never knew how exhilarating it was."

"So this was a good choice?

"The best," she agrees, bumping me with her body.

"You two are so sweet," the older woman says. "How long have you been married?"

"Oh, we're not married," Geneva says without missing a beat. "I'm just using him for sex."

The woman looks shocked as she moves over by her husband. I place my head in my hand. She laughs when I shake it.

"Geneva," I mumble. "She's kidding," I say louder. The woman just shoots me a dirty look. Her husband wags his eyebrows at me. "Can we not leave at least one older couple in the western United States unscandalized?"

"Nope," she says. "But you know you love me anyway."

"I do." She's kidding, but I'm not. It's why I've decided I can't just have a one-and-done with her. I love her too much to use her that way. I can finally admit it. If she wants to do this, I'm all in. I do want the house, kids, and a successful business. And I want it with her.

"Alright, everyone. We have more paddling to do before we're done for the night," Chuck says, and everyone piles back into the raft. Our guides load the trash in the cooler and set it in the boat. Soon, we're right back in the rapids.

By the time the raft pulls back up to the bank, everyone's energy is waning. We climb out and find our stuff. Geneva helps me pitch the small tent I brought. She arranges our sleeping bags inside while I fish out dry sleep clothes. We both have long underwear, socks, and watch caps to sleep in. It promises to be a cold one tonight.

Our guides cook dinner. We sit in a circle and eat out of bowls. Terry, our other guide, entertains us by singing camp songs. Many I know from all the times I camped as a kid. Geneva is enamored by them though. I forget that the idea of living in a tent and singing by a campfire is new to her.

Eventually, Chuck puts out the fire and we all head to our tents.

"Are you warm enough?" I ask as Geneva settles inside her sleeping bag.

"I will be. Just need to get settled."

"If you need anything in the night, just wake me."

"Okay. Thanks." The campsite grows quiet. Slowly, I drift off to sleep.

The next thing I know, I'm being woken back up by someone shaking my shoulder.

"Peter?" Geneva whispers.

"What's wrong?"

"I'm frozen. Can I sleep with you?"

"Of course." I unzip my sleeping bag and spread it out. Grabbing hers, I zip them together to make one big one. She snuggles underneath, next to me. Her feet are like ice. I can feel them through her socks.

"Put your feet between mine." She does as instructed and I pull her against me. Soon I hear her breathing even out as she drifts off.

I debate staying awake just so I can enjoy her body pressed against mine. No wonder the other woman thought we were married. Your friend usually doesn't share a sleeping bag. I tuck a lock of hair that's escaped her braid behind her ear. She murmurs and snuggles up tighter under my chin.

I already know this will be the best sleep I'll get. Something about having Geneva in my arms feels so right. If I can just convince us both that this could be our life.

My eyes close. She's safe in my arms for now. All is right in the world.

thirteen

GENEVA

TODAY IS the last day of the adventure part of our road trip. After a restful night snuggled against Peter's warm body, I'm ready to go. We pack our tent, sleeping bags, and clothes back in the dry bags and secure them in the raft. Terry feeds us a hearty breakfast full of carbs that I wolf down without a second thought. Then we're back on the water.

I close my eyes to take in the world around me. The water rushes under me, taking us toward the next rapid. Cold air caresses my face, turning my cheeks pink. Peter sits behind me with his paddle in his hand. His quiet strength reminds me nothing bad can happen as long as he's near.

My eyes open to feast on the scenery around us. This is life at its best. It's wild and free, and I want to live in this moment forever.

"Alright, rafters. Here we go," Chuck shouts as we enter whitewater. We fight as a team to keep our raft in the middle of the river. We cascade over rocks as we work together to victory at the other end.

A cheer rises from us as we clear the first set of rapids. Even Peter has gotten into celebrating the small victories. His deep voice makes my body shiver as it washes over me.

It's probably why I'm not paying attention as well as I should be when we enter the next set of whitewater. Everyone is tired today, even though we're excited to be back out.

I don't notice when Karen, one-half of the older couple, slips. The paddle comes out of nowhere. By the time I register it's coming at my head, it's already struck.

There's a moment of pain that shoots through my head. Then I'm in the water. It fills my mouth and nose. My only thought is that I can't lose consciousness or I won't survive.

My life jacket is no match for the current. I struggle to the surface, but the water is too fast. I crash against rocks as I hurl downstream. Right when I think I can't fight for even one more second, a strong arm wraps around me.

"I've got you.' His warm voice soothes me. I know at that moment I'll be okay. Even as the river tries to carry us away, Peter will protect me. I can give up the fight. Hand it over to him.

"We've got her," I hear vaguely as my mind swims back awake. I must have passed out. My body is being lifted out of the water and back into the boat. Hands tug me into the middle of the raft. I'm rolled to my side as water expels from my lungs.

"Peter," I rasp.

"I'm right here, sweetheart." The raft dips. Then he's pulling me into his lap. We're both dripping wet. A survival blanket appears from somewhere and he wraps me in it. His strong arms encase me as I shiver. "We need to get to a hospital," Peter growls.

"I'm so very sorry." I hear a watery voice whisper. It was an accident; I know that. "What can I do?"

"Get us down the river, now." Peter hugs me tighter. I can't seem to get warm no matter how hard he's trying. "Stay awake for me," he urges. It would be so much easier if he'd just let me sleep.

"Keep us straight," Chuck shouts. The raft suddenly picks up speed. I can't fight it anymore. My mind drifts to sleep no matter what Peter does.

The next thing I know, I'm being lifted out of the raft. My eyes open long enough to see Peter step into an ambulance, still cradling me against his chest.

Men cover me in blankets and push a needle into my hand. Warm liquid floats through my body. A light is shining in my eyes. It makes my head hurt. My wet clothes are removed before I'm wrapped in fresh blankets. I drift off again.

The light above my head is muted when I wake again. My hand grazes a bandage on my head. There's a noise at the end of my bed. A warm hand takes mine. I know the hand as well as I know my own.

"Peter?" I croak.

"I'm here," he answers. I force my eyes open. He's standing next to me in a pair of scrubs. "Fuck, Geneva. I thought I'd lost you."

"But you came to my rescue," I say. "Just like you always do."

"Just like I always will."

"What did Rand and I do to deserve you?" I ask.

"I always assumed I'm just another stray you kept." He smiles. I would like to say something snarky, something very Geneva-like, but my head hurts too much. "You get some rest. The doctor doesn't think there's anything wrong, but he wants you to stay overnight just to be sure." He straightens the covers over me. "I'll be right here."

I want to tell him to go back to the hotel so he can get some rest. That would be the smart thing to do. But I'm selfish. I don't want him to leave me alone. I want to scream at him to stay with me forever.

When I hear him settle back in the chair at the end of the bed, I'm struck by something I guess I've always known. Peter isn't going anywhere. Not without me anyway.

My mind plays tricks on me when I fall back asleep. Once again, I feel myself pulled under the water. No matter how hard I fight, I can't reach the surface. I look down to see why. My ankle is chained to the bottom of the river. I can't get loose. My lungs spasm as I try to hold my breath. It's no use; I'm going to drown.

An otherworldly voice tells me to just give in. To take that last watery breath. I can't, not yet. I still have too much I want to do. Too many mountains to climb. People I want to hug just one more time. I want my nephew to know who I am. I want to give Peter the chance at the love he deserves. But the river won't turn me loose. My fight is in vain.

"Shhh." I hear through the nightmare. "I've got you." The bed dips, and strong arms wrap around me again. Peter pulls me against his chest, and I press against him as the last vestiges of my dream evaporate.

"You're okay." He tucks the covers around us. My mind finds peace this time as I drift back off. For once, I'll let him be strong enough for both of us.

* * *

"Good morning," a doctor says, pushing through the door. I sit up, rubbing my sleepy eyes. The space next to me in the bed is empty. I find Peter standing across the room sipping on a coffee. "How are you feeling this morning, Miss Randolph?"

"Better," I admit. He listens to my lungs, checks my pulse, and shines his penlight in my eyes.

"Excellent. I think we can get you out of here. There isn't any damage, save for a small concussion. You're very lucky, Miss Randolph. Every year, people drown while rafting that river. I'll have the nurse bring your paperwork."

The doctor turns and shakes hands with Peter. They walk out together. Peter returns in a few minutes with another cup of coffee and hands it to me.

"Are you hungry?" he asks.

"Not really. I'm just ready to get back to that rainshower." He pulls clothes from a sack and places them on the bed. "How are these clean?" My previously wet, filthy clothes from yesterday are now freshly washed.

"I paid one of the orderlies to do it after his shift."

"Peter Winsloe. Making it rain and resourceful all at the same time."

He smirks at me.

"You couldn't exactly go home with your ass hanging out of the back of that gown," he says.

"Did you peek?"

"Of course." We grin at each other. Everything is going to be fine. "I'll wait outside while you dress."

I climb off the bed. When the door closes behind him, I quickly peel off the hospital gown. My leggings feel amazingly warm as I pull them on. I choose the heavy sweater to pair them with. He's even managed somehow to dry my boots. How much did he pay that orderly? I'm tying my last bootlace as the door swings open.

"Looks like you're ready to go," a nurse says, stepping inside. Peter is on her heels. She goes over the paperwork with us. After a couple of signatures, we're out the door.

I settle in the passenger side of the SUV to wait for Peter to walk around the hood. He wouldn't hear of me opening my own door. Or hooking my own seat belt, for that matter.

"I booked us another night here," he says. He starts the car, and we pull away from the hospital. "I think we can use a day off after that." I nod as I turn to stare out the window. I'm already sleepy again. Nothing sounds better than laying around our suite for a day. Peter thinks of everything.

We travel back in silence. Reaching the hotel, we climb the stairs to our room. The only thing on my mind is washing the river away with a long, hot shower.

I leave Peter on the couch. Turning the water as hot as I can stand it, I step into the spray. It beats down on my sore muscles, cuts, and bruises. I must look like a nightmare.

When the water has shriveled half my body, I step out. There's a mirror that runs the length of the wall behind the sink. With just a towel wrapped around my body, I stop to study myself in it. I've got new bruises on top of old ones. There's a scar where I had emergency surgery as a teenager. Several tattoos grace my torso, arms, and legs.

"I'm a disaster," I say to the man who's now leaning against the doorjamb. I was so anxious to get into the shower, I didn't close the bathroom door. "I mean, look at me. Who gets a mouse tattooed on their shoulder? Pathetic."

That was always my father's favorite word to describe me, pathetic. If you hear it enough, you begin to believe it. I let it harden me into someone everyone is scared of. I truly did become pathetic.

There's a growl behind me. In two strides, Peter has his hand wrapped around my throat. I'm pressed against the counter, looking in the mirror. He looms over me from behind. His head ducks to kiss the mouse sitting on my shoulder.

"Is this the mouse I trapped in your apartment while you stood on the table?" he asks.

"Yes."

"Is this a quote from the book of poetry by Robert Frost I gave you on your eighteenth birthday?" He holds up my arm so I can see the script that runs down my forearm. "I thought you said it was stupid?"

"Not so stupid."

His other hand traces a spot under the towel on my hip.

"Is this the boat we hid in from your father that night?"

I nod.

"And did your father teach you that word? Pathetic?" I try to look away from the mirror, but he tightens his grip on my throat. It's not enough to bruise, but it catches my attention. "Look at me." Reluctantly, I do.

"Do you want to know what words I see you as?" He waits until I nod again. "Beautiful, smart, fierce, strong, brave, sexy. Do you need me to keep going?" I shake my head. "I will keep telling you what I see until you believe it yourself. Who do you think knows you better, me or your father?"

"You," I whisper.

"Damn right, me." He leans down until his lips are almost touching my ear. "Now, my beautiful, smart, fierce, strong, brave, sexy woman, get dressed so I can feed you." He releases me and sweeps from the room.

I take a moment to regain my equilibrium. How does he do that? How does Peter send me so off balance I can't remember which way is up?

"Now, missy," he barks from the living area. I jump and quickly pull on my clothes.

He doesn't realize it, but I can't get the smile off of my face. It'll take years for him to make me believe his words. But I'm beginning to think I'd like to stick around until he does.

fourteen

PETER

MY GRANDMOTHER once used the word trifling to describe my brother and me. I'm beginning to understand what she meant. Geneva is nothing if she's not trifling.

I worried that her nightmares would come back last night. They must have, because she climbed into bed with me in the wee hours of the morning. Apparently, we're now sleeping together, just not "sleeping" together.

She was already gone when I woke up this morning. I found her sipping on a coffee near the windows in the restaurant downstairs. After everything, she still stares at the view like it takes her breath away. I slide into the seat across from her.

"Look who finally dragged himself out. I thought you'd decided to become a gentleman of leisure," she says. Her eyes twinkle with a spark of her usual mischief.

"My bed got cold," I say.

"Hmmm. I bet we can think of something to heat it back up," she purrs.

"Behave." I smile. It's nice to see Geneva feeling her oats again. "How's the head?"

"As hard as ever." She holds up two fingers to a passing waitress. A steaming cup of coffee is placed in front of me. I order breakfast before she hurries back toward the kitchen.

"No headache?"

"Only the one sitting across from me." She winks at me over the rim of her cup. "What are we doing today?"

"What would you like to do?" I ask.

"Honestly?"

"Always."

"I think I'd like to leave."

"Do you feel good enough?" I study her face. Do I see the effects of a concussion? I should argue that we need another day to recover.

"I just think the nightmares won't leave until I move on," she says. "I love it here, but I'm ready to go."

"Okay." I can't argue with that. The nightmare she had in the hospital almost undid me. By the time I realized what was happening, she was terrified. All she'll tell me is they involve drowning. "I wish I hadn't booked rafting."

"I don't. It was beautiful and freeing and something I wouldn't have passed up regardless of what happened. Accidents are going to happen no matter what we do." She stares out the window again. "I wouldn't take back one second of this trip."

"Not even the couple's message?"

"Especially not that," she says with a laugh. "It was worth every second listening to him scold you when you squealed over your glutes. Even a drunk, topless kiss was worth it. I just wish I could remember it."

"I'll draw you a picture when I have time," I tease.

"Would you? Be sure it's suitable for framing. I'll put it in my new office."

"I'm sure your brother will appreciate that."

"We can only hope he's brutally scandalized," she drawls.

We finish our breakfast and head back upstairs to pack. I was able to slide our room in Santa Fe a day early. It'll be dinnertime by the time we arrive, but at least we have a place to stay. I carry our bags downstairs. Geneva disappears in the gift shop while I check out. She meets me by the SUV with a sack.

"Guess what they had?" she asks, pulling more magazines out of the bag.

"Seriously?"

"Yes, we have a long drive." She opens the first one as I pull away from the hotel. "Let's see, what do we want to start with? We already know you don't have a type and you're good in bed. Though you admitted that the first time wasn't so great." She flips several more pages. "Here we go. Is he marriage material?"

I groan. When I planned this trip, I envisioned her spending hours reading in the car. Or at least working on a crossword puzzle. Never would I have thought we would play twenty questions about my love life. I should have bought that license plate game I saw in the toy section for her.

"Question one. What's his job situation and income?" She raises an eyebrow at me.

"You know exactly what my income was. Now it's nonexistent, and the job prospects are iffy at best. I'm just hoping my two partners can pull their weight this time."

"Not nice," she says, hitting me on the arm with the magazine. "You know you're going to be just as wildly successful as always. Rand said he's already getting contacted by several prospects wanting you to work on their projects."

"They're probably just after my sexy business partner," I tease. "You're not too bad either."

"Question two," she continues, glaring at me. "What does he do when you take him to a family event? Lord, that's a loaded question."

"I've always behaved around your family. Well, for the most part. There was that time I convinced your brother to streak across campus with the rest of the team. Oh, and that time I called your dad an asshole to his face. Hey, but your mother likes me."

"Did she ever flirt with you?" she asks.

"No. Why?" There's no way Rose Randolph would ever be inappropriate with a minor. Even as an adult, she barely acknowledges my existence. That doesn't stop me from teasing Geneva though. "Wait, you mean I could have had mother and daughter? At the same time?"

"Keep it up and I'll have you pull this vehicle over. You can walk the rest of the way." Her eyebrow cocks at me again. At least I know she's not lying to me about her head. Geneva with a headache is less teasing and more stabby. "Does he rely on you when he needs help?"

"All the time."

"He never needs help," she exclaims at the same time.

"What do you mean? I need help sometimes," I insist.

"Name once."

"You rubbed the aches out after Yosemite."

"Yes I did," she says. "Damn, that ass."

"What about when you flew all the way to Virginia for my grandmother's funeral? My ass wasn't involved that time."

"In my world, your ass is always involved," she quips. "But I knew how close you were to your grandmother. I couldn't imagine not being there."

"It meant a lot." She smiles. That weekend was the first time I realized there was more to her than she let the world see. She missed two days of college classes just so I'd know she cared.

"Does he do what he can to make your life easier?" She rolls her eyes. "Ummm, how about convincing me to go into business together, helping pack my apartment, carrying me down a mountain on his back, and sitting on the back of a horse for hours so I don't have to be uncomfortable?"

I don't know how to respond. Of course, I do what I can to make her life easier. I've even gone so far as buying tampons to drop off on the way by. What kind of man would I be if I didn't?

Certainly not the one David and Tricia Winsloe raised. My dad taught me everything I needed to know about how to treat a woman. At least the ones I didn't use as a one-night stand. He doted on my mom at every turn. Tim and I learned through example.

"Can he stay calm in a crisis? Seriously? He pulled me from a raging river before I drowned. How much more of a crisis do we need?"

"It was instinct."

"Fucking good instincts, I say," she points out. "Has he cooked you dinner? About every night."

"I like to cook." I'm not sure why I'm defending myself. I like cooking for Geneva. She's the only person I ever cook for. Not even Rand gets my french toast.

"Well, I love your cooking. So, win-win. Can he handle conflict?" She studies me closely. "I think he handles conflict like a hostage negotiator. As a matter of fact, he should probably yell more before he develops an ulcer."

"Do you want me to start yelling at you?"

"Only if it includes apology sex after," she says.

"Who's apologizing?"

"You, of course. I never do anything that needs apologizing for."

"Mmmm." I can think of a time or two that an apology would have been nice. She once knocked me down the fucking stairs at work with a hip bump. I guess she made sure I was still living before stalking off.

She also announced at the dinner table when we were kids that I was obviously inbred since I hailed from the hills of Virginia. My mom is a schoolteacher. My dad is a hospital administrator. We're not inbred. I don't even know anyone who is.

"Last question. Are you compatible in bed? Well, that's a shame. We almost had our answer." She cuts her eyes at me. "I guess now we'll never know."

"Are you trying to bait me?" There's no question we'll be compatible in bed. "What do you want me to do to you in bed?" That came out wrong, but I am curious.

"Let's see. The choking thing you did last night was nice," she says. "Biting and spanking are still on the table. Some bondage should do the trick. How are your knot-tying skills, Boy Scout?"

"You're just trying to get a rise out of me." She takes a slow perusal down my body until her gaze reaches my lap.

"Looks like I already have."

I can feel my face flame bright red. You'd think it wouldn't embarrass me anymore. The fact she can turn me on just by speaking isn't exactly a secret.

"Just sit there and read your book," I mumble, and she

laughs. But she has pity on me and pulls her book from her door pocket.

"Do you want me to read out loud to keep you awake?"

"Is it one of your banned romances?"

"Of course."

"Then, no thank you. My jeans are tight enough as it is."

She laughs again. Opening her book, she settles in to read.

There's a small smile on her mouth. Thankfully, the near-drowning hasn't seemed to have affected her too much.

I don't understand why she can't see how strong she is. Not many people can come away from that without suffering adverse effects. She seems to have just chalked it up to another life experience.

It's dark by the time we pull into Santa Fe, New Mexico. I don't know what it is about this town, but I've always loved it. One of the first projects Rand and I worked on was here. I got to know my way around pretty well in the weeks I spent working. The hotel I chose sits right in the city center. We'll be able to walk to everything.

"This is lovely," she says as we pull into one of the historic hotels.

"Let's check in," I say. "Then we'll find somewhere to eat we can walk to."

"That sounds perfect. I'm ready to stretch my legs."

We climb out of the SUV. I grab our bags while she collects our coats. It's turned cold here. The check-in process is easy. We're shown to our suite in record time. Leaving our bags, we walk back down to the lobby. After getting several recommendations for dinner, we head out.

"Ohhh, it feels good to get out of your car for a while. What are you thinking you want to eat?" she asks.

"Southwest. What else?" She loops her arm through mine as I steer her across the street. "I haven't had a good bowl of posole in a long time."

"I'm on board as long as it heats me up."

I pull her against my body to keep her warm. My arm drapes around her shoulders. She doesn't elbow me in the ribs like she would have just a week ago. Instead, her arm wraps around my waist.

I'm tempted to lead us around town for a while just so I don't have to let her go. She's cold though, so I lead us just one more block to the restaurant. We're led to a table.

"What's the plan tomorrow?" she asks once we're seated.

"You wanted to shop. Art, jewelry, clothes, anything you want."

"Careful, Peter. You'll make me come with all that foreplay."

"I've got plenty more where that came from."

"Umm," a waiter who can't be out of high school says. "I'll come back." He skitters off like he's on fire. I'm not sure we'll see him again tonight.

"Peter Winsloe," she chides. "You really should learn to behave."

"If I don't, will you spank me later?"

"Don't make offers you can't keep."

"Oh god," the waiter says next to our table. So he did come back. We can't help it; we burst out laughing. Now we're scandalizing the next generation. Does that mean we've moved up?

I watch as Geneva placates him by placing a drink order. She winks at me, and all I want to do is yell how much I love this woman. I'm in trouble.

GENEVA

IT'S STARTING to snow when I step outside the restaurant. Peter is still inside, settling the bill. I've offered to pay several times, but he just scowls at me.

The streets are nearly empty. I'm sure everyone is holed up inside. The streetlights highlight the fluffy flakes as they drift to the ground. The scene is surreal and beautiful.

Stepping out into the empty street, I stick my tongue out. I laugh thinking of all the times Rand and I did this very thing on our occasional ski trips growing up.

Those were always the best weeks of the year. My father stayed home to work, so it was just the three of us. We would terrorize the slopes while my mother sat curled in front of the fire, reading to her heart's content.

"Take a picture, perv," I say to the man leaning against the arch in front of the restaurant. I knew the minute Peter stepped outside. Call it a disturbance in the force. My body just feels it when he's near. A photo flash snaps in my face.

"Thanks," he teases. "My spank bank was running low."

I laugh. Peter can always make me laugh. He's also made me rage, cry, and feel way more over the years than I'd like to admit. In some ways, I think that's what love is. To hand a piece of yourself bit by bit to another person, trusting them not to destroy you. I've fallen in love with Peter Winsloe. It's the most terrifying thing I've ever done.

"Come help me catch snowflakes," I say. He pushes off the wall to join me in the middle of the street. He leans his head back and opens his mouth. I have a moment to take in the muscled column of his neck. He laughs before looking back down at me. Our gazes meet. Then his lips are on mine.

His lips are cold from the night air. His tongue, though, is warm when it slides inside my mouth. He tastes like cinnamon from the dessert we shared. My hands grab the front of his coat. His hands smooth through my hair.

I want to stay like this forever, in the middle of the street, in this place. I don't want to keep going; for the fantasy to end. I don't want a life where he'll grow tired of me.

He stands back up, his stormy gaze sweeping over me. His brows are furrowed as he studies me like I'm a puzzle that needs solving. I can almost see the war waging inside of him. There's no point in me trying to sway him. He'll make the decision he thinks is right, damn the consequences.

"Come on," he says, finally taking my gloved hand. I almost have to jog to keep up as he drags me down the street. He nods to the receptionist as we move through the hotel lobby. We step into the elevator and he's on me again. His body is hungrier this time. His tongue is more urgent. With a swish, the elevator doors open, and he steps back.

His keycard is ready when we reach the room door. I'm

pulled inside roughly. Peter locks the door and strips out of his outerwear. Then he strips me out of mine. With one more calculated gaze, he lifts me to his waist. My back is pressed against the wall.

"I've reached my breaking point, Geneva," he growls. "I can't just stand back and watch anymore." His lips crash against mine.

My hands find the buttons of his shirt, scrambling to get the buttons open. He breaks our kiss only long enough to rip it over his head. My nails sink into flesh as he presses me harder into the wall.

Suddenly, I'm being carried into a bedroom with a king-size bed. Peter is not gentle as he tosses me onto it. He follows me down, making short work of my shirt. His gaze stalls on the clasp of my bra.

"I know you've seen a front closure before," I tease.

"Not one of yours." His hand flicks it open. My breasts tumble out. He gently strokes the hard peak of my nipple like it's something to be cherished. His mouth replaces his finger, and I arch at the pleasure that shoots through my body.

"Peter," I moan. My hips buck against the thigh wedged between mine.

"Shh, little mouse. I've waited a long time for this. We're not rushing through it." His words make me moan even louder. I reach for the button on his jeans as his lips kiss a trail to my other breast. This time, he doesn't shove my hands away. My fist closes over hot flesh when I have his jeans opened enough. His hips rock as my hand becomes slick with pre-cum.

Then he's gone as he works down my body. I want to scream in frustration for him to come back. That I wasn't finished with him. But he's very much in charge, and he wants something different. My pants are dragged down my legs and discarded.

"I like these," he says, playing with the soaked intersection of my panties. "But they're in the way." Twisting his hand in the waistband, he rips them from my body. There's a new pulse of heat making my body even slicker for him. "Better," he says. Then I feel his tongue take a long, slow journey through my lips.

"Peter," I beg.

"Mmmm" vibrates from somewhere in his chest directly to my clit. I become shameless in a heartbeat. I can't get enough of what he's doing to me.

I roll my hips, riding against his face. His strong arm presses my hips into the mattress as he continues. Not being able to move is both excruciating and exquisite at the same time. My body begins to vibrate as my orgasm sneaks up on me.

"Peter!" I scream as I come undone. He gives me no quarter as he wrings every vestige of pleasure from me.

"I like when you scream my name," he says, placing one last kiss on my mound. I'm too exhausted to answer. He climbs back up my body until he's gazing at me. "Doing okay?"

I nod my head. It's all the energy I've got.

"Then I have a question," he says.

"Yeah, what's that?"

"How dirty do you want it?"

My mouth goes dry. Suddenly I'm not as tired as I thought I was.

"As dirty as you want to give it to me, Winsloe." My chin juts toward him in challenge, and his eyes narrow. I think this is about to be a wild ride.

"Okay," he says. "Wait here a moment."

The bed dips as he climbs off me. He disappears down the hall, where I saw our luggage sitting briefly.

My mind whirls imagining what he has in mind. Should I go to the bathroom just to make sure I can last? How many orgasms is he going to insist on? I've had men that can do multiples. This is far from my first rodeo. What does Peter have that the rest haven't? Other than my heart.

"Stop overthinking it," he calls from the other room. I snort and flap my arms on the bed. He chuckles as he reappears. Even though his hands are full of stuff, I focus on what's missing. He's removed every stitch of clothing from his body. His cock stands proud as he stalks toward me.

"Condoms," he says, tossing a handful on the night-stand. I quirk an eyebrow at him. That's a lot of condoms. "You said you wanted it dirty, not reckless," he says in answer. "Now, get on your knees."

"By the way," I say, flipping over and pushing up to my knees. "Condoms are optional. I'm on birth control, and I know we're both clean."

"How do you know I am?" He straps a collar around my neck.

"Because I know you haven't had sex in at least six months."

"I could have been sneaking around," he points out. A spreader bar is hooked to my ankles.

"You're horrible at keeping secrets. You haven't been with anyone since you took home that blond from the year-end banquet." He pulls me to my knees and places my hands on the headboard. I feel his body press against mine as he leans his mouth next to my ear.

"I only fucked someone when you announced a new boyfriend. It never helped though. All I wanted was this tight cunt." He slaps me on my mound, wringing a gasp from between my lips. "Let's see what I've been missing."

He pulls the collar tight against my throat. Fresh heat surges through my body. His fingers slide through my folds against the sensitive bud. As hard as I struggle, my legs are held open. A tingling sensation begins everywhere his fingers find.

"What is that?" I ask.

"You'll find out," he answers. "Tell me if I do anything you don't like. I'll stop immediately." Of course, he will. This isn't some random hook-up I've brought back to my room. This is Peter, my best friend. I relax and rock against his fingers. He'll never do anything to hurt me. "Ready?"

I brace myself for what's about to happen. A blindfold slides over my eyes. Have I ever told him how much I love to be blindfolded? I rarely trust anyone to do it, however.

I shiver as his lips gently suck on my neck. Teeth replace lips; a slick cock replaces fingers. I rock my hips back, begging for more. My ass is met with a stinging slap.

"So hungry," he mumbles. The tingling turns into a raw need as the tip of his cock slips inside me. I don't know what he used on me, but it's turned me into an insatiable animal. I want him to fuck me right now. Hard and deep.

"Peter," I demand. I try to grind my hips against him, but he moves with me. He's keeping me from impaling myself on him. "More."

"Behave, Geneva," he hisses with a slap to my ass. "I'll let you have a little more when you act like a good girl."

"Asshole," I sneer.

He laughs. His cockhead jumps inside me. I take a deep breath and relax. He rewards me by rocking his hips. Delicious pain pushes pleasure through me. He's large, and I haven't done this in a while. He was right to make me wait.

Slowly, he begins to thrust. He gets deeper with every one until he's buried inside me.

With every rock of his hips, I feel my body buzz with my impending orgasm. Then I hear a vibration. His hand snakes around my body. The vibration rests against my clit, and I explode. Colors swirl as my body screams out. Or is that me screaming?

He doesn't let up. My orgasm is barely through my system before another follows in its wake. I can't breathe, even though the collar has been removed from my neck. If I could just close my legs, I could control what he's doing to me.

"Bad girl," he says with another strike to my ass. "Almost made me come before I was ready."

My ankles are freed from the shackles holding them in place. I feel him pull my hands away from the headboard. He has to pry my fingers off one by one. I'm eased back onto the bed, cradled in his arms. My blindfold is removed. I blink in the dim light.

"More?" he asks. My body begins to heat again at that one simple word.

"Yes," I say shakily. How do I want more? My head tells me to climb on him and ride like there's no tomorrow. My heart tells me to never let him go. Drawing on what little strength I have left, I swing my legs around until I'm straddling him on the edge of the bed.

"Take what you want," he says.

So I do. I slide my aching cunt onto his hard cock. There's a sheen of sweat on his forehead as he leans back on his hands and thrusts his hips up. I test how far I can rock up without losing him. Then I ride back down, relishing in the fullness.

My eyes feast on every part of him. The way the muscles

bulge in his neck. How his eyes glaze over like a sea in a storm. Then I watch as we come together, sealing our fates.

"Fuck," he sighs.

"Yes, several times," I agree.

His gaze stares back into mine. I wish I knew what he was thinking. Would the world end if I told him I was in love with him? He doesn't move, so neither do I. We sit, just looking at each other, until he finally softens. Now we just have to figure out where we go from here.

sixteen

PETER

I'VE BEEN PLANNING this since I was old enough to dream about fucking Geneva. She's dated acrobats and artists, both more creative than I am. It's why I've traveled across the United States with toys in my duffel. If I can't be bendy or broody, I can at least be domineering.

The sexual pleasure-enhancing oil was just an added bonus I picked up on one of my business trips. Amazing what those folks in California can do with a few simple ingredients.

Geneva sits on my lap, staring at me. Her skin glistens with a fine sheen of sweat. Those green eyes are half-lidded with exhaustion. I didn't think I rode her that hard. It was just an introduction to everything I have planned for her body. Hopefully, I didn't mess her hair into a knot. I know how hard it is to brush the tangles out.

She lets out a sigh and slumps against my chest. Her soft curves press against me. Just the thought of her perky, nude breast has me half-hard again. My hand strokes up her back.

"Come on, sweetheart. We need to get that stuff washed off you. Neither one of us wants to be found dead in this room tomorrow from a sex heart attack." She moans, so I stand with her in my arms.

I leave the lights off in the bathroom so she doesn't have to blink at the brightness. Turning on the water, I wait for it to heat before stepping into the shower.

"I'm going to have wet hair to sleep on," she says.

"Then put it up while I hold you out of the water."

She pulls her hair on top of her head. Wrapping it around into a knot, she secures it with the band she wears on her wrist. I've watched her put her hair up a thousand times. It never gets old. I'm mystified every time by how she keeps it up there.

"Maybe, before we wash off whatever that devil oil is you used," she says. Her eyes open, and she spears me with a mischievous gaze. "We could get one more ride in." She wiggles in my arms until she'd lined up to my already hard cock. Slowly, she slides down until I'm encased by her warmth. "How does that still feel so good?" she moans.

"It's us, Geneva," I say, sliding my hands under her ass. "We were always going to feel this good."

"I guess this answers the sexual compatibility question."

"Let's hold off on that until we run a few more tests," I suggest.

She laughs, and my cock jerks. I won't last long this time since I slipped the cock ring off a second ago. If you think I could have lasted through sheer willpower the first time she came, you're insane.

The one now sitting on the soap dish at my elbow I had

custom-made. It's made of brass and has her name on it. I figure if I have to wear a collar, it might as well be one I picked out.

"Peter," she screams before clinching around me hard enough to pull me along with her. My hand slaps the shower wall to steady us. Spots flash in my eyes as lava burns up my spine. I don't understand how I can keep coming this hard. Slowly, I set her on her feet. I can't be relied on to keep us both standing after that.

"So, I know I said one more," she pants. I've created a monster. I just hope I remain her victim of choice.

* * *

She holds me to two more before I'm finally allowed to turn off the shower. At this point, I can barely see straight. My cock has given up on me, and Geneva is asleep before she even crawls in bed. We agreed that pajamas were too much trouble. It's why I find her sweet, naked body curled around mine the next morning.

"Are you ready for some shopping?" I ask.

She moans, kisses my cheek, and rolls out of bed.

"Or we could do something about the morning wood," I call after her.

"You do something about the morning wood," she snaps.

"That's not as fun."

"Neither is the beating my den of iniquity is complaining about."

Den of iniquity? She has more names for her sex than a dog has fleas. I've heard most of them over the years as we bantered back and forth. This is a first for this one though.

"My rod of Asclepius would be happy to look into that for you."

"You're ridiculous," she says, walking out of the bathroom. "What is this?" She holds open her hand. Resting on her palm is my cock ring. "I mean, I know what it is, but why is my name on it?"

"Because I've always belonged to you. I might as well have your name on me."

"How long have you thought about this?"

"About us? Since we were old enough to fuck."

"This, Peter. How long have you had this ring? Have you fucked other women with it on? Because that's a whole other plain of messed up."

"No. I've only had it about a year, which was the last time I was with anyone else." Her eyes narrow like she doesn't believe me. "Do you remember when I came to the office with a shiner? You'd just taken up with that douche from the country club."

"Cooper?"

"Yes, the guy with the yuppie name. Well, I found some random woman to take home from a bar. Only problem was I slipped and called her your name instead of hers. She cold-cocked me in the face." I've scooted up to rest against the headboard. She glares at me for a minute before bursting into laughter.

"Please tell me you didn't."

"I did. That's when I decided to stop dicking around and wait for you."

"Was this whole trip a plan to seduce me into bed?" Her eyes glint with laughter. I don't think I'm actually in trouble. Yet.

"Not neccessarily."

"Peter Winsloe," she says, batting at my chest. "I don't think I even know you anymore."

"Yeah, you do. I'm the same guy. Just with benefits now." She laughs and leans in to kiss me. I turn her simple peck into something a lot more salacious.

"Nope," she says, pressing me back against the head-board. "You promised shopping."

I pout at her.

"But," she continues, "if you're very good, I might have a few tricks of my own to show you later."

"From your lips to God's ears."

"Oh, I'm sure I'll be singing his praises later too. But, if you don't get dressed, you're going to meet him soon. I'm starving."

"Yes, ma'am," I say with a salute.

"Remember that for tonight." She sways into the other room to dress, and I head for the bathroom where I hurry to get dressed. I know one thing for sure: a hungry Geneva is an angry Geneva. She gives new meaning to the term hangry.

When she emerges from the other bedroom, she's dressed in a sweater dress, tights, and a pair of fuzzy boots I've never seen.

"You look beautiful," I say, standing from the couch.

"Thank you." Her smile lights up her face It makes my heart skip a beat. Is this what it's like to be a boyfriend? The last real girlfriend I had was in college, and we were never that serious. I wonder what Geneva would say if I asked.

I know I should be beating myself up for even thinking of her as my girlfriend. What happened to all that bullshit about not sleeping with your best friend's sister? It went up in smoke the second I found her outside, catching snow on her tongue. I saw through the attitude to the woman she deserves to be. One with no fear of the future. I had to claim her as mine.

It's not fair to hold someone to a promise made years ago when you're young. Rand made me swear to leave his sister alone the day she started working with us. I was only twenty-two at the time. There were plenty of women in the sea.

Now I'm older and much wiser. I understand that there is no one else like Geneva, no matter how hard I search. Rand is just going to have to get over it or look elsewhere for a best friend.

The first thing we do is stop for breakfast. She nibbles on a pastry while I have the full Southwest American breakfast. It's similar to the full British one, only the beans are better. She watches me spoon a sizable helping of them into my mouth.

"So much for not farting during sex," she says. It takes everything I have not to blow beans all over the table.

"I told you it was an impossible requirement." She rolls her eyes and takes a sip of coffee. I toss my spoon back onto my plate. "Now that's all I'm going to think about."

"Did I just ruin sex for you?" she teases.

"Nothing could ruin sex with you, sunshine."

"Nice cover." She laughs. "We should probably go before we upset any more serving staff."

"That wasn't even our best material." I toss enough cash on the table to cover our bill and a generous tip, just in case. We walk outside, back into the cold air.

Soon we're lost among the many art studios around Santa Fe. Geneva has always loved art. Her office was filled with it. Everything is now packed away in boxes as it travels across the country.

"Oooh, I love this," she says. She's looking at a stylized

piece that can only be described as folk art. I know why she likes it though. The colors are vibrant. They draw you in, the way she does with me. I check the price on the wall next to it. They're not giving it away, but I can afford it. I motion to the clerk.

"Can you ship this?" I ask when the woman approaches us.

"We'd be happy to."

"You can't be serious," Geneva says.

"Consider it an office warming gift." She gawks at me. "From your boyfriend?" We'll see how violent this reaction will be. She mulls it over for a minute. Then, grabbing the front of my shirt, she pulls me in for a kiss.

"I'll say a proper thank you later," she mumbles against my lips. A voice clears next to us.

"So, can I start the paperwork on this piece?" the woman asks.

"What do you think?" I ask with my arms still holding Geneva against me.

"Definitely," she answers. I nod, and the woman scurries off to a desk in the back. "Boyfriend, huh?"

"I was trying it on for size."

"Does it fit?"

"Pretty damn well, I think."

"Hmm," she hums. Her fiery gaze meets mine. "I guess we'll find out."

Find out, my ass. I tried it on and found that it fit like a glove. I'm willing to risk everything for this. I won't fight for my stake in our new business if Rand wants me out. I'll go, but I'm taking her with me. She takes my hand when we step out of the gallery.

"Boyfriend sounds so teenage," she says. "I think it needs a better name. Hmm, let me think." She pulls me inside another gallery. Her voice lowers. "How about boy toy?"

"No."

"Penis-enhanced arm candy."

"What? That's a definite no. I think boyfriend is fine." We wander through the artwork before stepping back outside. There's a café across the street that looks perfect for lunch. We're shown to a table and order before Geneva picks back up our conversation.

"I know. Zaddy."

"By all means, call me Zaddy in front of your brother. That should go over well."

"Fine. Boyfriend." She scowls. "So boring."

"I like boring; it's nice and simple."

"Except you're anything but boring or simple," she says. "At least not in bed."

"Just wait until I bring out the big toys."

"You had me at big...Zaddy."

seventeen

PETER

I'VE ALWAYS THOUGHT window-shopping was pointless. Why spend hours browsing with no intention of buying anything? That was until the first time I went with Geneva. Somehow, she turned it into a blood sport. It's now a great way to spend a day listening to her eviscerate store after store.

"All I'm saying is, they would sell more by changing the color palette in the store. Nothing about chartreuse says 'please buy my cardigan.' Unless it's ripped, spray painted, and makes you want to rage against authority," she says, walking out of the latest shop. "They had some good stuff in there too. But, eww." She does a little shimmy to show her opinion of the assault to her senses.

"So I take it I should tell the painters to pick another color for the new office?"

"You don't have to worry about that. Brontë and I have already agreed on a color palette."

"Do I dare ask what color my office will be?"

"You dare not," she says. "I want it to be a surprise. You should see the new logo I'm designing. It says young, edgy, but still traditionally elegant." She uses her hands to make her words look like they're on a marquee. "What are you smiling at?"

"You," I answer, taking her hand. "I knew we were making the right decision."

"Right decision about what?"

"About making you the head of operations."

"What?" Geneva gapes at me. Rand, Brontë, and I discussed last month our roles in the company. It was unanimously agreed that Geneva is the most obvious choice to keep the train on the tracks. No one else can fill the role like she can. "Why?"

"What do you mean, why?" I ask with a snort of derision. "Because, G, you're brilliant. You're organized, goal-driven, and have a way of making people give you what you want. That's on top of how fucking genus you are at the advertising. You already have branding ideas, for Christ's sake. None of the rest of us have even thought about it."

"I just assumed I'd keep doing what I did before at Randolph Development." We've stopped in the middle of the sidewalk. Good thing it's not the height of shopping season. I'm not sure why she's so surprised by what I've said. To us, she is the obvious choice.

"No, you're going to be in charge of keeping this whole shitting-shebang going. Rand will still buy properties, Brontë and I are going to do the design work, and you'll have to run the business. Oh, you still have to do all the stuff you did before as well."

"Okay. Well." She stares down the street in thought. "I guess I should start putting in some overtime then. There's a lot that needs to be done." We head back toward the hotel. "I think I'll start with kicking Rand into a smaller office." The wicked smirk is back on her face. The look I love so much. "I mean, should I even be sleeping with someone that's beneath me?"

"Beneath you? Definitely. Sleeping? Not so much."

"Speaking of, what do you think about ordering in tonight? That way I can just lick it off of your abs."

"Damn. I can't say no now."

"I know. You're way too infatuated with me to ever say no."

"That I am."

* * *

I have to admit, I'm a little disappointed. We ordered dinner in, but nothing has been licked off my abs yet. Geneva sits across from me at the small table in our suite, waving her fork around. She's finished her salad and has moved on to a piece of carrot cake.

"I'm telling you," she says between bites, "there's no way that something that contains carrots and nuts can have this many calories."

"Keep dreaming, Randolph." I'm one to talk. I chose a fat piece of chocolate pie for dessert.

"I don't care what you say; this stuff is to die for. Besides, why eat salad if it's not so you can have cake after? I mean, no one voluntarily lives on roughage." She pops another bite in her mouth. She clamps her lips around the fork and pulls it slowly out of her mouth. I'm at half-mast just watching the show. "What time do we need to leave tomorrow?"

I calculate the time in my head. It's a solid ten-and-a-half-hour drive to Austin from here. The snow started again a little while ago, so I doubt we'll make great time getting there. If we can get somewhere that is about halfway, I'll be happy. There are only two ways to get there. Either way, we should be good.

"How about we aim for seven? The sun should be up by the time we're done with breakfast."

"Perfect," she says, pushing away from the table. "That gives me just enough time to do very nasty things to you and still get plenty of sleep."

"Very nasty, huh?" I just went to full mast.

"You heard me, Winsloe. Now get on the bed."

"Yes, ma'am." I don't have to be told twice. Pushing away from the table, I head to the bedroom. I sit on the end of the bed to wait for further instructions.

I used to tease Rand that his sister would make an amazing dominatrix. He was never amused by that observation. It still made for an amazing fantasy. Hopefully, that fantasy is about to become reality. What can I say? I like a woman who takes what she wants.

"Let's see what you have in this thing," she says, carrying my duffel into the bedroom. "Take off the shirt," she adds. I pull it over my head and toss it on the floor. She digs through the bag. "Rope!" Her eyes gleam with glee. "Lay down with your arms over your head."

I lay back and raise my arms over my head. No one has ever tied me to a bed before. Trust was never a thing with a one-night stand. The last thing I wanted was for housekeeping to find me the next morning naked in a bed.

Truth is, I bought the rope with Geneva in mind. She pulls out a length of yellow. With surprising proficiency, she has my arms secured to the headboard in minutes. I raise an eyebrow at her.

"Rand taught me all his sailing knots. I practice when I

get bored." She shrugs. "Now, what to do with Peter Winsloe." Her nails stroke down my chest to my abs. I can't stop the shiver that races up my spine. "He's been such a bad boy teasing me all these years." I might be in over my head.

Her hands land on my waist. Slowly, she unhooks my belt and pulls it from my belt loops. When it's free, she loops it so the ends are in one hand. I watch in fascination as her other hand traces the leather to the looped end. Then she cracks it. The noise echoes around the room.

"Geneva," I warn.

"Did I say you could talk?" The belt slaps gently against my chest, but I jump anyway. She drags it down until it snakes between my legs. Her fingers pop the button of my jeans open. I hear every tooth of my zipper unlock one by one. "Shall we see whose name is on your cock tonight?" My jeans are slid from my legs.

"Yours. Always yours," I groan.

"Do I take your word for it, or do I find out for myself?" She eases my boxer briefs from my body. "Geneva. Very nice. You need a reward for being such a good boy." Her lips close around the head of my cock, and my breath catches in my chest. "Mmm," she hums. The vibration goes straight to my balls.

My belt is looped over my cock. I close my eyes, waiting for whatever sweet agony she has in store for me. I'm wrong. Her mouth draws on my cock as she pulls the belt slowly. When the end hits the floor, she slides until I'm pressing the back of her throat.

The tingling in my spine begins. I focus on tamping down the need to come back down. It's no use with her pouty mouth working me.

"I'm going to come," I warn. Her lips pop when they pull off me.

"No, you're not," she says, stabbing me with her emerald gaze. "Not until I tell you to." She stands to pull something from the bag. As hard as I strain, I can't lift my head far enough to see what it is. The bed dips, and she's straddling me. "How bad do you want me?" she asks.

"Fuck, Geneva," I moan. "I can't think of anything I want more than that sweet little pussy. It consumes me." I'm rewarded with a smile as she slides the belt around my throat. I don't even care anymore if she kills me with it. I just need to feel her fucking me more than I need air.

"Beg, my dirty boy," she purrs.

"Please, Geneva." The belt tightens as she rises to her knees. Inch by inch, she sinks until she impales herself on me. She takes a couple of trial bounces. Then I realize what she's had in her hand this whole time. It's the small bullet vibrator I bought her. It presses against my rim as she leans back on top of me.

"Geneva," I beg again. My body sizzles as she seats the vibrator where she wants it. "I'm not going to last."

"You'll last until I say differently," she snaps. The belt tightens a little more. I can breathe, but I'm starting to feel a little light-headed. Her hips grind up and back as she rides me.

I can hear myself whimpering, but there's nothing I can do to stop it. There's nothing I'd want to do anyway. I've never been brought to the edge like this.

Her breathing becomes shallow as she chases her orgasm. I'm teetering on the brink of oblivion when she shouts at me. "Now, Peter." I come harder than I ever have. Somehow, I'm still on the bed but also floating above it.

Geneva looks like an angel and temptress rolled into one as her head snaps back in ecstasy.

"Peter," I hear her calling. My eyes open to find her still sitting on top of me. The belt is gone, as is the buzzing in my ass. "Did I kill you?" She leans over me to untie my arms.

"Possibly." My heart is still slamming in my chest. She rubs on my numb arms to help wake them up.

"I think you're going to have a mark on your neck," she says, scrunching her face up. "Sorry."

"I fucking hope so. Otherwise, I might think I dreamed all of this."

"You did come really hard," she says with a laugh.

"I don't know how you didn't get knocked against the far wall."

"Hence the belt." She winks. I use one rubbery-feeling arm to pull her in for a kiss. I'm not sure there's much else on my body that is working.

Her naked breasts crush against my chest, and I start to feel stirrings again in my groin. She breaks the kiss to look at my lower body. "So, I'd guess we give it ten before you're ready to go again?"

"Mmm, maybe five? Seven tops."

"You know, this thing is growing on me." I hope she's talking about my cock. Instead, she eases the ring off of me. "Maybe I'll have your cock tattooed with my name."

"No, I draw the line at cock tattoos."

"Hmmm, your hip then?"

"That we can talk about," I agree. "Maybe in a nice script."

"In several languages," she adds. "That way no one will be able to claim they didn't know who you belonged to if they get your pants down."

"Now you're getting carried away. Everyone who gets in my pants can speak English." I pull her against my chest again. If I have to wait another five minutes before I'm on her again, she can damn well wait with me. "How much time do we still have before bed?"

"I'd say somewhere around two hours," she says.

"We'd better hurry then." With one quick move, I roll her under me. "I still have lots of toys waiting."

GENEVA

I DON'T KNOW what I was imagining, but sex with Peter is perfect. He's not afraid to push the limits, but he also likes it slow and intimate. Like this morning when I woke up with my leg hooked over his hip and his cock inside me. The slow grind while he gazed into my eyes was more emotional than anything I've experienced before. It was almost on another level.

"Wow, it's really starting to come down," he says, walking up behind me. I guess I'll have to store my thoughts of sex with Peter until later. I've been standing outside for a few minutes now, wondering if we'll get out today.

"It is," I agree. We're standing under the overhang of the hotel. "Do you think we'll be okay heading out?"

"I think so. It's odd to have snow this early. The desk said it shouldn't be this bad once we go farther south."

"Okay, then."

I step out into the snow toward the SUV. Peter follows

me with our bags. I made sure he had the bag of toys when we checked out. Don't want to leave that one behind. He stores our bags in the back, and we both settle inside.

"At least we shouldn't have to fight any traffic," he points out. He starts the car and we pull out of the parking lot. The snow hits the windshield. Peter turns the wipers up another notch. I watch as Santa Fe disappears behind us in a blanket of white.

We ride in companionable silence for miles, both of us lost in our thoughts. I'm studying Peter out of the corner of my eye when I see him yawn. My only real job on this road trip has been to make sure I keep the driver awake. He insists on driving, so I've settled for being the entertainment.

"Guess what time it is?" I tease, reaching behind me for a magazine.

"What quiz could possibly be left? We already know you're my type, we're both going to be awesome spouses, and I'm more than adequate in bed," he grouses.

"You're better than adequate."

"You're more than adequate, too. You're a freak in bed." I smack him with the magazine. "I didn't say I didn't like it."

"Anyway, back to the quiz. It's a would you rather one," I say. "Would you rather accidentally text nudes to your parents or butt-dial them during sex?"

"Come on. What kind of a question is that?" He stares out the windshield at the blowing snow as he thinks about his answer.

"I guess the nudes. I might be able to warn them in time before they open the text. I don't know. Once they figured out what was happening on a butt dial, they should hang up the phone. That's a damn choice, either way. Just the thought of Mom listening to us having sex is enough to give me nightmares."

"I'd want to butt-dial my father. Then I'm going to scream your name over and over so he knows exactly who I'm fucking. That should induce a heart attack."

"Harsh," he says with a laugh. "I appreciate you included me though."

"Would you rather walk in on your grandmother having sex, or would you rather she walk in on you?"

"Ahh, if Grandma Winsloe was still alive, I'd be all about her getting some. But I don't want to see it. I'll have to pick her walking in on me. She liked you too, so I think she would have been okay with that."

"Thank you," I say. "I just met your grandma Winsloe once, but I think it would be better for her to walk in on us too. Though we could save everyone a lot of drama with a few bedroom door locks."

"You make a good point."

"That's very true. Moving on. Would you rather only be able to have sex in the shower or on the floor?"

"I'm not sure. We've done both. What did you prefer?" he asks.

"Well, I like the water aspect, but most accidents in the home happen in the bathroom. Makes sense to avoid that. The averages are against us."

"I see your point. If you're already on the floor, there's no chance of falling. So we're safe saying we vote floor?"

"Absolutely," I agree. "Would you rather your best friend marry your dad, or would you rather you were allergic to sex of any kind?"

"Rand can have my dad," he says. "I'm not giving up sex for some stupid allergy. It'll just make family holidays a little more awkward."

I throw my head back and laugh. The thought of straight-laced Mr. Winsloe hooking up with my brother is absurd. Looking at Peter, I find him grinning too. He's well aware the chances of that are less than zero percent.

I take a minute to appreciate how his eyes light up when he laughs now. Something inside him has changed. He doesn't scowl like he used to. Even though this is the most ridiculous quiz so far, he's laughing at it with me.

"I like this look on you," I say.

"What look is that?"

"Me. I like the way I look on you."

"So do I. Very much, especially from my back."

I shake my head. The man is crazy, but I haven't managed to erase the smile off my face. I never knew being with Peter could be so easy. I flip several pages of the magazine. Is it just my imagination or has it grown darker in the SUV? Glancing at the windshield, I find the snow coming down even harder than before.

"Is it my imagination, or has the storm kicked up?" I ask.

"No, it's definitely coming down harder than when we left."

"So much for the storm letting up the farther south we get. I can barely see off the front of the hood." I check my phone to see if I can figure out where we are. There's no service. "I can't get any service, or I could check the weather."

"Yeah, there's not much out here. We'll pull off in the next town. Maybe we can find out what it looks like for the rest of the day."

I nod and gaze back out of the windshield. My magazine lies forgotten on my lap. It seems frivolous to be interested in some ridiculous sex quiz when Peter is white-knuckling the steering wheel. The best choice is for me to remain quiet so he can focus on driving.

"Any idea where we are?" I know, I promised to be quiet. But it's eerie outside. It feels like we're all alone in a horror movie. With the darkness surrounding us, it looks like fog as thick as soup. Peter slows down even more as the wheels slip on the ice that is forming. We need to get off the road.

"I'd guess somewhere near the Texas border, but I'm not positive," he says. "Shit!"

I turn back to the windshield just in time to see what he's looking at. A huge deer is standing a few feet in front of the Rover. Its antlers stretch out from its head like a forest. I grab the door rest as we begin to slide. The SUV misses the buck by inches as we careen off the road.

We stop in the ditch, inches from a fence this time. My heart is pounding in my chest hard enough that I'm sure Peter can hear it. We're lucky that all four wheels are still on the ground. It would have been easy to flip over as we slid.

"Are you okay?" Peter's voice is frantic.

"I'm fine. Nothing hurt."

"He came out of nowhere," he says. "He stood higher than the hood. I didn't want to hit him and take a chance on him coming through the windshield."

"No, I agree." We both sound slightly hysterical. I'm sure it's just the adrenaline dump.

Peter nods and places the Rover back in drive. He presses the gas pedal. Nothing happens but the sound of wheels spinning. He fiddles with the instrument cluster before trying again. We get the same result.

"Mother—" He ends with a frustrated sigh. "Wait here, I'm going to see if I can figure out what the problem is." He pulls on his coat and opens the door. The wind is blowing so hard, I'm hit by snow before he can slam the door closed.

I watch as he investigates the front of the car and then moves toward the back. I unhook my seat belt so I can kneel on the seat to follow him. He keeps shaking his head. That can't be good.

"Is everything okay?" I ask the minute he drops back into the driver's seat. He sits for a moment before answering me. My anxiety amps up a thousandfold.

"I think we're stuck," he finally says. "The ground must have already been muddy when the snow started. Between the ice and mud in the ruts, it can't get any traction."

"What do we do?"

"Do you have any service?" We both check our phones. I shake my head in answer. "Yeah, me either. Well, we'll just hunker down here until someone comes along. We have plenty of warm clothes and sleeping bags."

I don't ask all the questions swirling through my head. What if no one comes and we freeze? What if the wrong person comes? What if he hurts us, or worse?

"Are your true crime podcasts getting in your head?" he asks.

"A little," I admit.

"We'll be fine. I promise."

A weird thing happens. I actually believe him. Peter hasn't let me down yet. If a mountain and a river couldn't get me, a little snow isn't going to either. He turns the engine off. Leaning over the front seat, he begins rummaging through our stuff.

"Here, slide into your sleeping bag." He hands it to me. "It's going to get cold fast. When we can't stand it anymore, I'll start the Rover up to get some heat. I don't want to take a chance on running out of gas though." He pulls out my gloves, hat, and scarf too. I dutifully pull them on before wiggling into the sleeping bag.

"Do you think we'll be here long?" If we're going to be here in this dim car for hours, I need to figure out how to stave off boredom. That and keep my mind off of random serial killers.

"I don't know."

"So—" I'm fishing for something, anything to talk about.

"So," he says, reading my mind. "I'd like to hear more about this wedding between my dad and your brother."

"You know it would be beautiful," I say with a laugh.

"True. My dad cuts a decent silver fox in a tux."

"And my brother looks like he could be on the cover of *GQ*."

"Yeah, if Joseph Randolph did nothing else, he did pass down some good genes."

"David Winsloe didn't do so bad himself. Do you think if we had kids, they'd look like Keats?"

"Are you offering to find out?" he teases. "Maybe he does look like Rand. I'd be good with the girls looking like you. Though, I'd have to keep a bat handy by the front door to beat the boys off."

"But not to keep the girls at bay? You know they can be just as bad."

"I can't exactly take after some woman with a bat. I'll leave you to deal with them."

"How old are we talking before the kids are allowed to date?" I ask.

"I'd say at least thirty-five, maybe forty." I laugh. "The girls anyway."

"That's a double standard."

"Absolutely. But no nasty man is going to tie one of my

precious daughters to the bed and fuck her while I'm around."

"So that only works when your wife is involved?"

"Now you're starting to understand." He grins at me. I know he's teasing. My daughters will be strong, independent women who will know how to get what they want out of life. Why are we even talking about our hypothetical children in the first place?

A fist knocks on the window and we both jump. Peter steps out of the car. I can see a man in a jacket with a patch on the arm. Do killers wear patches on their clothes?

I watch as they walk to the front. They both bend over to look at something. They straighten up, still talking. Finally, Peter walks back to the driver's door.

"We're getting a ride to town. I'll get our bags and come back to help you. Button up your coat."

"Wait," I say. "How do we know he's safe?"

"Well, I don't think highway patrolmen usually make skinsuits out of people. I guess it's possible, but we'll just have to take our chances."

I breathe a sigh of relief as he closes the door. Checking my phone, I find we've been sitting here a lot longer than I thought. Hopefully, someone in town can help us get on our way. A hot meal would be welcome at the very least.

"Ready?" Peter asks, opening the door again. I finish zipping up my jacket, grab my purse, and climb over his seat. The cold hits me like a sledgehammer. Peter helps me slide across the patchy ice until I'm deposited inside the patrol SUV. The officer has the heat running on high.

"I'm glad I was doing one last sweep before heading in for the night," the officer says. "Deputy Gonzales," he continues, extending a hand to me. "You can call me Mateo."

"Thank you so much, Mateo. I can't imagine spending all night out there," I say.

"It would have sure been a cold one," he agrees.

"Can you take us to the nearest hotel?" Peter asks from the back seat. "I can call a tow truck to pull us out tomorrow."

"I'll arrange a truck for you," Mateo says. "Afraid the hotel is all booked up because of the storm. I might have an idea of somewhere you can stay though."

"We'd be grateful," Peter answers.

"Of course. Now hang on, folks. This is going to be a heck of a ride."

nineteen

PETER

I WASN'T CONCERNED where the officer took us as long as Geneva had heat. The longer we sat, the tighter she pulled the sleeping bag around her. The idea of spending the entire night in below-freezing temperatures was not something she needed to do.

Everything in the small town we finally reach looks closed for the weather. I should have paid closer attention to the forecast.

"This storm seemed to have come out of nowhere," Mateo says, as if sensing my self-recrimination. "Caught us all by surprise. Well, here we go." He pulls up in front of a small cabin in the middle of nowhere. "My brother-in-law said you can use it as long as you need."

At first look, there doesn't seem to be much to the building. It's an old bunkhouse that's been converted into a hunting cabin. There's a small porch with a slick-looking set of steps. The handful of windows are covered with what looks like burlap. I guess we can't complain. This is our only choice, and it was beyond generous to offer it to us.

"This looks perfect," Geneva says. It doesn't sound like something she would say. I love her, but in the past, she would have found a thousand reasons we couldn't stay here.

"Yes, thank you," I added. Opening my door, I step into the cold. Mateo helps with our bags as Geneva slides carefully to the door. It opens and a tall, thin man greets us.

"Come in, come in. It's cold enough to freeze the balls off a brass monkey out here," he says. "I got the fireplace going. There's extra wood in the room off the back door in case you need it. The missus sent me with some supper for y'all. She's no slouch in the kitchen."

"Thanks, Gene. I reckon they'll be fine. Come on, let's leave them to get some rest," Mateo says. "Dee said he'll get your truck as soon as it's thawed enough to pull it out. Stay warm."

"Thank you." I shake both men's hands as they head for the door. I lock the door behind them and walk to Geneva, who's warming up by the fire. "Are you doing okay?"

"Yeah, I'm fine," she says.

"I'm sorry we've wound up here," I say. I could kick myself for ever leaving Santa Fe in this weather. I honestly thought we'd drive out of it shortly. The front desk even assured me we would. Never did I think it'd get worse.

"This has been a crazy trip, hasn't it?"

"I won't argue with you on that," I say. "You might not want me to plan our trip next time."

"I disagree. I wouldn't have missed this for the world. Look at everything we've done. I hiked Yosemite, rode a horse through Zion, rafted the Grand Canyon."

"Almost drowned," I point out.

"Won money in Vegas," she continues, ignoring me. "Bought a painting in Santa Fe. Finally had sex with my best friend." She bats her eyes at me. I move closer to her.

"I like that last one the best."

"Me too. I also don't mind staying in this cabin in the middle of a snowstorm. At least for tonight."

"You would have a month ago," I point out.

"That was before my best friend showed me there was more to life. Believe it or not, I wasn't very happy with my life before. Unfortunately, I took it out on everyone around me. It's still a hard habit to break."

"I know," I say quietly. "You don't have to change who you are though."

I've known for a long time that Geneva wasn't happy. How could she be with her father reminding her how worthless she was every day?

She was in a job that didn't allow her to grow to her potential, and it got worse after her brother left. It's why I convinced her that we needed to leave. I blamed it on helping Rand begin a new chapter in his life. But it was for her.

"Why wasn't I happy?"

"Because you were never allowed to be. Rand and I can tell you that you deserve more until we're blue in the face, but you needed to see for yourself." I pull her into my arms. "You've just discovered something I've known for years. You truly can do anything you set your mind to."

"You always say the perfect thing." Her lips press against mine.

"That's because I love you," I murmur against her lips. She pulls back to study me. Her gaze stares into my soul. "If you think it's too soon to say that, it's not. I've loved you for a long time."

"I don't think it's too soon. I think I've loved you for a long time too. It was just too terrifying to admit it even to myself," she says. "I never believed love was something that lasts. Now, I want to believe it does. That there are people that live their entire lives in love with that one special person. That it never fades. I want to find out what that feels like."

"Then that's what we'll do. We'll simply stay in love forever."

"Just like that."

"Just like that," I say. She wraps her arms around my waist and squeezes me to her.

"How about we check out what kind of a cook Gene's missus is?"

I know when Geneva needs a break from her emotions. I've seen love that endures, but it's all new for her. I need to proceed carefully. Someday she'll finally be able to believe love can persevere.

"He did say she's no slouch in the kitchen," she says.

"Ringing endorsement if I've ever heard one."

I take her hand as we walk into the small kitchen. It's more like some appliances at one end of the room. There's a bed in the corner and a sitting area by the fireplace. The only other real room I see is a small bathroom between the kitchen and bed.

There's a large casserole dish sitting on the counter. It's surrounded by a carrier with hot packs surrounding it. Opening the lid, we find a meat-slash-noodle concoction that smells heavenly. There are dishes in the only cabinet next to the refrigerator. Geneva piles several spoonfuls on two plates. We return to the seats by the fire to eat. She curls up on the couch next to me.

"Okay, this is fucking amazing," she says between bites.

"Do you think it's really this good, or are we just that hungry?"

"Doesn't matter. At this point, I might trade you for Gene's missus."

"We could be a threesome. I wouldn't mind having someone else cook occasionally."

She grins at me before digging back in. I'm not ashamed to admit that I polished off two plates worth before slowing down. Gene did not lie. Geneva sits back and groans. She finished her entire plate of casserole. For her, that's a lot. She's used to picking at her meals.

"Get enough?" I ask.

She cuts her eyes at me.

"There's still some left."

With another groan, she rubs her stomach.

"Should I take that as a no? There's cobbler over there too."

"Oh, god." She turns to look at the counter. "Just a small bowl."

I laugh and stand. Scooping out two small bowls of what smells like peach cobbler, I return to the couch.

"This smells amazing. Damn that Gene's missus."

We finish up our cobbler and set the bowls on the coffee table. I need to build the fire back up. I haven't seen a thermostat anywhere in the small room. Taking the poker, I work on settling the logs before adding more. Geneva lays her head on my lap when I sit back down.

"This is nice," she says. "I wouldn't mind staying here for a while."

"I guess we know where we're vacationing next year."

"Or the beach. I have a new swimsuit I'm dying to try out."

"I'm good with that. Apparently gray is all the rage in men's suits."

She laughs. She does it all the time now. It's music to my ears. Geneva sits up and swings around until she's straddling my lap.

"You know the best thing about this cabin?"

"What's that?"

"The bed is right there," she answers. She leans forward and tugs at my earlobe with her teeth. My cock stirs awake. She gives a slow roll of her hips.

The bed feels a million miles away. Geneva tugs on my shirt until she gets it over my head. Her hands run over my chest like she's discovering it for the first time.

I take my time with her shirt. My body heats with each button I unhook. Her creamy skin pebbles with gooseflesh when I push it off her shoulders. My fingers trace the strap of her bra over her shoulder. They wrap in her long hair. I pull her to me, not able to keep my lips from hers for even one more second. She tastes of sugar and cinnamon.

My hands find the clasp on the back of her bra. Her breasts are freed for me to caress. I weigh them in my hands, marveling at how her nipples harden with just one swipe of my thumb. I graze my tongue over one, and she moans in response. I love how sensitive she is.

"Are you set on the bed?" I ask.

"No." She stands from my lap. "I'm not necessarily pro-bed." With a shimmy, she pushes her tights down her legs. If I had known she wasn't wearing any panties, I would have forgone Gene's missus's casserole.

She takes on the fly of my jeans next. I lift my hips so

she can slide them to my ankles. She kneels over my thighs and slowly sinks onto my cock.

Wrapping my hand in her tresses, I kiss her like she's the very air I breathe. Her body works me closer to the edge, her hips rocking as she grinds deeper. I won't last long. I wasn't prepared for this. There's no cock ring to hold me back.

"Peter," she moans. I'm taken by surprise when her pussy clamps around me. She pulls me with her as we orgasm together. This is more than just sex. Geneva feels it too as she rests against my chest. "I love you," she whispers.

"I love you."

* * *

GENEVA

I'm starting to think of time as divided into two segments. Before waking up with Peter wrapped around my body and after. The room grew cold sometime in the night, but snuggled against his body, I'm toasty warm. I never knew waking up with a man still in my bed could be so nice. Especially when one of his best assets is nestled against my ass.

I stretch, and he mumbles a protest behind me. It's a habit I'm starting to get used to. Scratch that; it's a habit I am used to. Do I have to give it up when we reach Austin?

My new apartment will seem empty without Peter taking up the extra space. Will we still hang out in the evenings together like before? Can I seamlessly turn my best friend into my lover without losing what we already have?

"I can feel the wheels turning in your head." His voice is rough with sleep.

"Just thinking."

"About?"

"How all of this is going to work when we hit Austin," I answer.

"Jesus, Geneva. It's too early to be stressing over something we can't answer yet. That's the beauty of being in a relationship. We can figure it out together as it happens." I roll over in his arms. His eyes open to spear me with a sleepy gaze.

"How would either of us know how a relationship works?"

"Look," he says as a smile spreads across his mouth. "All I know is I want to be with you. I'll deal with the rest of it later."

He gives me a quick kiss and rolls out of bed. I watch as his gloriously naked body disappears into the bathroom. He reemerges in his sweatpants, hung low on his hips. Crossing to the fireplace, he pokes at the ashes. He coaxes the fire back by adding fresh wood to the embers.

"I'm just saying we need to make a plan." I push up against the backboard. The sheets are wrapped around my body. I'm not shy either, but it's still cold in the room. "Are we taking turns staying in each other's apartments? Do you want to even sleep over? How long do we wait to tell everyone? That's all I'm saying."

"Mmm," he says. Crossing the room, he pulls me back down the bed by my ankles. Stretching under the covers on top of me, he braces on his forearms so he can gaze directly into my eyes. I can feel his manhood pressing against my heat.

"Or we see what works for us and let the chips fall

where they may," he says. "Now it looks like I have at least an hour before I have to be dressed. Maybe we can find a better way to distract that beautiful mind."

His lips lower to mine. The cock that was calm a second ago now grinds in all its glory against me. He's right, my mind settles. There's time to worry about the future later. All I want right now is to be in the moment with Peter.

twenty

GENEVA

PETER'S SUV shows up on the back of a tow truck around noon. We've been dressed for hours. I've washed the now-empty casserole dish, and we've played a hundred rounds of gin rummy with the only deck of cards in the cabin.

There's not much else to do here. You don't realize how much you miss technology until you don't have it. Our phones still have no service, and the cabin doesn't offer internet.

"Let me grab some cash to pay you," Peter says to the large man standing just inside the cabin door.

"Nah, I'll just bill ya later. Write your email on the ticket. My wife does the billing between wrestling kids," he says. "That way, y'all can get on your way. The roads are cleared for the most part."

"Okay. Well. Thank you." Peter doesn't know what to say to that arrangement any more than I do. Is this how every small town handles life? No wonder Rand moved to Dansboro Crossing.

Peter follows the man outside to help get the Rover off the truck. I make one more sweep through the cabin before settling on the couch to wait.

"Ready?" Peter asks, walking back inside. It's only been fifteen minutes, but without phone access, it feels like hours. "Are you just staring at the fireplace?"

"Maybe."

"Okay. I guess we'd better get back to civilization before you start having withdrawal symptoms." I flip him off over my shoulder. He's not offended, judging by the laughter. Then again, he has seen that finger a lot over the years. "I guess if you think there's time."

"Is sex all you think about?" I stand and shoot him a glare.

"Every second of every day," he quips. I cock a hip. He grabs our bags. With a sigh, I shrug into my coat and follow him out the door. Sometimes he just doesn't rise to the bait.

I notice a wad of cash lying on the counter in the kitchen. Figures that Gene didn't charge us for the cabin either. Peter's a man who pays his debts though. He would have thought about that casserole and added extra.

"Holy shit, it's cold," I complain when the wind hits me. The tow truck is sitting farther down the driveway, with exhaust pouring out of the back.

"He's showing us how to get back to the highway," Peter says, following my line of sight. "Here, get in." He holds the door so I can clamor inside. The seat warmer is already on high. He tosses the bags on the seat and climbs in beside me. "Buckle up. The roads are still icy." The tires crunch on the ice as we follow the tow truck down the winding driveway.

He leads us all the way into town before flashing his lights to let us know we're on the right road. Peter spies the lone diner with its open sign in the window. We agree that we'd rather make miles than spend time inside waiting for our food. He runs inside and returns with two sandwiches. What makes me happiest is the carrier of coffee.

"I'm not sure what we wound up with," he says, handing me the bag.

"Looks like ham, bacon, and cheese." I fold the paper on one of the sandwich bags so Peter can hold it without taking his eyes off the road.

Pulling the other sandwich out, I sink my teeth into the gooey goodness. What is with this town? Is it a secret pocket of gourmet chefs? I guess we will never know as we put miles between us and it.

"These people can cook," he points out.

"I was just thinking that. There's a bunch of fries in the bottom too." I pop one in my mouth. It's still hot and just salty enough to be good. "I couldn't live here. I'd be the size of a house."

"We'd have that in common, for sure."

Speaking of, surely I can find at least one last quiz in one of the magazines. I reach into the back for my stack. Flipping through one, I find a quiz that should be a little more light-hearted than what we've been doing.

"When I ask you a question, just say the first thing that comes to mind. Whatever your preference is, okay?"

"Okay," he says hesitantly.

"Dog or cat?"

"Dog."

"Yeah, I would guess you're a dog person. I don't care either way. I like dogs and cats. Would you rather go out or stay in on Friday night?"

"Yes," he answers.

"That's not an answer."

"Yes, it is. I'd rather take you out for the evening, then head home and spend the rest of the night on top of you. I guess if I can only choose one, I'll take on top of you."

"Would you rather vacation in the mountains or on the beach?"

"After this, I'll choose the beach. With you in that bikini."

"We should go dive off the wrecks around Florida next time. I'll wear the bikini."

"Deal," he says, offering to shake my hand. I take it, and he pulls my knuckles to his lips. It's a very boyfriend move.

"Let's see. Would you rather move back to your home-town or never go back?"

"I like where I grew up. I'd move back if I had to, but I'm not itching to. It'll be nice to live closer though. Maybe I can see my family a little more often."

"I love San Francisco, but I feel the same way. I'd rather live closer to Rand than my parents. I'm sure I'll go back for a visit eventually. Not any time soon though," I say. "Would you rather have no kids or eight?"

"Eight," he answers without even hesitating. "I grew up in a large family. My siblings were the best part of that."

"You just made my uterus scream in fear," I tease.

He throws his head back and laughs. Why is it not weird to be talking about our future kids constantly? I guess I'm starting to feel invested in this relationship. I have to admit, I like the way that feels.

"Ooh, this is a good one," I continue. "Do you prefer a quickie or to take your time?"

"I don't think that's a fair question. There are too many factors involved. Do we only have time for a quickie? Where are we? If we don't hurry, do we take a chance of being discovered? Or is it a lazy Sunday morning and we have all day? See, too many variables."

"Are you already planning sex in the supply closet at the office?"

"Absolutely. We're also having sex on Rand's desk, then just hinting about it so it drives him crazy wondering."

It's my turn to laugh. Peter and Rand have spent their entire adulthood torturing each other. They're closer than most brothers, which I'm convinced is why they do it. "Would you rather invest in experiences or objects?"

"Experiences," he says.

"Huh, I thought being an architect you'd answer objects."

"I'm more interested in the experiences the people that occupy those spaces have. If it's a historical building, I envision the people in the past and how they used the building. It influences my design decisions."

"See, I just learned something new about Peter Winsloe," I say. "Here, you thought these were a waste of time. Psst. Would you say you're more passive or confrontational?"

He's quiet for so long that I begin to give up on getting an answer. I've seen him let things I would pitch a fit over roll off his back. I've also seen what happens if you back him into a corner.

What I've never seen is Peter remaining silent when someone takes a shot at one of his friends. There's been more than one occasion when he came out swinging. We even got tossed out of a bar years ago because someone called me a bitch.

"How about this one? Are you more logical or emotional?"

"Probably emotional, as hard as I try to be logical. I don't know. Maybe I don't know myself as well as I thought," he says.

"I do. I'd say you're passive until you see an injustice. Then you confront the problem regardless of what it is. I also like that you feel so deeply. Sometimes you've had to feel for both Rand and I when we were too scared to.

"You're introverted no matter how hard you try not to be. It's obvious you prefer your drawings to people most of the time. And as much as you want to go with the flow, you like the structure of knowing what's ahead."

He glances at me with wary eyes.

"That's why I call bullshit that you're not already worried about how this relationship will go. You think you're the only one that can see into someone's heart. Make no mistake, I've seen yours for a long time."

"What do you think you see?" His tone is a challenge.

"I see a man who values his family and friends above all else. Who charges into the rescue with no concern for himself. I also see how easy it would be to hurt a man like that. One that feels his emotions so deeply that he will wait a decade for what he wants. You have always been the best of us, Peter. And I love you for that."

The car grows quiet. I don't know if I've pissed him off or not. I close my magazine and toss it into the back. No more quizzes, possibly ever. I study him as he stares out the windshield. We left the ice miles ago. The only thing in sight now is miles of flat desert grassland.

"I love you too," he says. His hands grip the steering wheel with purpose, but his eyes slide to mine. "The wait was worth it."

"It was," I say with a laugh. "I just wish we had done this earlier."

"I guess we weren't ready yet. I still don't know what I'm going to say to your brother."

"I vote we wait a while." He doesn't answer me. I know he likes things out in the open, but I want to keep this to myself just a little while longer.

"If that's what you want," he says quietly.

"At least for now."

I stare out the window as the miles click by. I don't ponder why I want to keep us a secret. That feels like too much baggage to unpack right now. The drama of the last couple of months is all I can deal with at this moment. Any more might send me over the edge.

"Do you think we'll get to Austin tonight?" I ask a few miles down the road.

"We should. There's not much between here and there anyway."

"Good." We ride in silence for another mile. "Will you stay with me tonight?"

"I can do that," he says with a smile. I smile back. Yep, I can grow old with this man. "Are you getting hungry? I know I could use a break."

"Famished. What are you thinking?"

"Nothing that takes too long if we're going to get there before midnight."

"Hey, look." In the distance, I see a giant sign in the shape of a W. "One last burger before I revert back to the world of quinoa and kale?"

"What the lady wants, the lady gets."

"I like the way you think, Winsloe. Keep it up and you might get a bonus for finishing this trip on time."

"I like the way *you* think, Randolph." He pulls into the parking lot and shuts off the engine. "Now get the lead out. I need that bonus."

"Tell you what, I'll throw in some extra incentives if you get me extra pickles," I tease. He hurries around the SUV to open my door.

"Let's go." He takes my hand. "I've got a restaurant worth of pickles to buy."

He pulls the door open and ushers me inside. I find us a table while he places our order. That's one of the perks of being in a relationship with your best friend that no one tells you about. He knows exactly how I like my burger.

twenty-one

PETER

EVEN WITH RUSHING Geneva through the Whataburger somewhere near Lubbock, we still don't make it to Austin before midnight. She's tucked against the window, sleeping soundly. I don't know how she does that. I've never been able to fall asleep in a car. It took me years to finally learn how to sleep on an airplane.

I weave through the downtown streets, hunting for her apartment building. I think I was in it once. It was one of many we looked at. The building might look familiar, but I can't for the life of me remember anything about the apartment itself.

Finally, I pull into the entrance of the parking garage. Punching in the code I have stored in my phone, I watch as the chain gate opens. It was one of the few things I insisted on. There's no way I would take a chance on her getting jumped in a dark parking garage.

I weave up the ramp to her assigned space on the

second level. Her car is already waiting for her, thanks to Rand.

Pulling into the guest slot next to it, I turn off the Rover. She doesn't stir. As much as I would like to sit here so she can sleep, we both need to stretch out on a bed.

"Hey, sweetheart. We're here."

"Really?" She stretches and sits up. I love it when she's still sleepy. It's like watching a kitten wake up. She rubs her eyes and pops the door open. Slowly, she climbs out before stretching the rest of her body.

"I'll grab the bags." It's becoming a daily mantra. We've packed and unpacked so many times now, I don't know how I'll handle being in one place again.

My arms are loaded down as I follow her through the doors to the elevator. Her apartment is crowded with boxes when we step inside. At least the furniture is in place. I'm sure we have Rand to thank for that too.

"I'll see if the bed is made," she says with a yawn. She takes her bag and disappears into the bedroom.

I need something to drink first. The refrigerator doesn't have much, but there are a few bottles of unopened water. Cracking one open, I finish it in one try. I leave the bottle on the kitchen counter since I don't see a trash can anywhere. Geneva hasn't made a reappearance. I pull a bottle of water out of the refrigerator and head for the bedroom.

I guess the bed was made after all, as Geneva is curled up under her comforter. There is a pile of clothes next to the bed where she undressed. I walk into the bathroom to find her personal items spread across the counter. Quickly, I brush my teeth and add my clothes to the pile and crawl into bed next to her.

She moans when I pull her back against my chest. After wiggling around for a minute, she finally sighs before settling back to sleep. Looks like we've already solved the problem of sleeping arrangements in our new city. I don't care where we lay our heads as long as we're together.

"I love you," I whisper. She doesn't answer, but then she doesn't have to. I already know what's in her heart.

With a last kiss to her temple, I pull her even closer. I drift off in our new city, safe in the knowledge that we've finally arrived exactly where we need to be.

* * *

The next morning, I wake to the sound of gears grinding. Geneva has found her stationary bike. By the way it sounds, she's got a demon on her tail.

I moan and roll out of bed. The pile of clothes has been tossed into a hamper in the bathroom. Fresh towels hang on the bars. There's soap and shampoo in the shower. How long has she been up?

"Have to make up for that last burger," she pants when I walk into the living room. She's pulled the bike next to what should be the dining room window. I watch her stick her ass in the air as she pedals. I've barely managed to shower, and she looks like she's training for a marathon. There's no way I'm burning off the calories from a trip that ended at one this morning.

"Should we make an appearance at the office today?" I ask.

"I'd say yes. Rand has already texted this morning to see where we are."

"What did you tell him?"

"That we'd see him this afternoon. No reason to tell him we're shacked up in my apartment," she says. "He said something about dinner tonight after."

I can feel the acid in my stomach at the thought of keeping what we're doing from Rand. It's not right, but I need to give Geneva the time she asked for.

I can't think of the last time we had a secret between the three of us. What about his wife, Brontë? She's not stupid. She'll guess what we've been doing right off the bat. I'll have to figure out how to avoid her as much as possible.

"Whew," she says, turning off the machine. "That felt good. I'm heading for the shower."

She pats my chest on the way to the bathroom. I shuffle to the kitchen. When did she have time to find the coffee pot? Doesn't matter. I pour myself one into the largest mug I can find. I can't remember ever drinking coffee from something that says "Don't make me cut a bitch" on it. I guess when in Rome.

I've almost finished when she walks out of the bedroom with nothing but a towel on. Suddenly, I can think of a lot better ways to spend the afternoon than at the office.

"Do you mind if I meet you at the office later? I want to get this place at least livable." That crushes that fantasy.

"Yeah, I need to see if everything made it to my place anyway." I cross the room to pick up my shoes. Sitting on the couch, I pull them on. "I'll sort through the Rover and bring your stuff to the office."

"Perfect," she says. She seems different than yesterday in the car. I hope she's not already regretting us being together. I thought I'd have more time to convince her this could work before she got cold feet. "Okay, I'll see you at the office," she says and walks back into her bedroom.

I finish tying my shoes and stand. I've been dismissed. I'm too tired to stomp into her bedroom to find out what this is all about. I'll get to the bottom of it later.

Picking up my duffel, I slip out of the apartment. My

Rover is right where I left it. That bodes well for easing my mind about Geneva's safety.

Climbing in, I start the SUV. Now to remember where my apartment is. I chose to be farther out of downtown. She might like the hustle of being right in the thick of it, but I prefer a little more solitude. Besides, there's a river running through the south side of town. Why wouldn't I want a view of it?

It takes me ten minutes to reach my place. Grabbing my bags from the back, I ride the elevator to the top of my new building, and I open my door and toss my bags inside.

The first thing I see is exactly what sold me on this place. A large bay window looks out over the river. There's a reason I splurged on the penthouse. First, the view, but more importantly, I plan on being just as wildly successful as I was before. With our combined business know-how, this new venture should soar. This place will remind me of that goal.

Walking into the bedroom, I find my bed has also been made. I bet money that was more Brontë than Rand. He lucked into a good one when he found her. Who would have guessed a one-night stand would turn out to be the one? Mine certainly never have.

I return to my living room and slump on the couch. I'll get around to setting up my place eventually. Tomorrow sounds soon enough.

I'm just getting comfortable when my door buzzes. I should have waited to submit my approved visitor list until I'd been here a while. With a sigh, I open my door.

"Hey, you made it," Rand says, stepping inside.

"Barely."

"I'm honestly surprised to see Geneva didn't feed you to some bears along the way. Beer?" he asks, handing me one from the six-pack he's carrying. He places the rest in my refrigerator, and we both return to the couch.

"She's not that bad. We had a pretty good time," I answer.

"Dude, you don't have to sugarcoat it for me. I know what my sister is like." I can feel my irritation starting to rise. There's no way I'll be able to sit here if Rand decides to bash his sister in front of me. "I'm glad it was a good trip though. I was worried when I didn't hear from you."

"We got snowed in. Besides, you know reception in the national parks is not so great."

"That's what G kept saying. I talked to her on the way over. It sounded like she was rearranging furniture."

"You know how she likes her feng shui." I tip the bottle back and swig half of it. "Where's Brontë?"

"She's at the office, fussing at the people finishing up the offices. I think she's nervous that you won't like it. So, please, rave about it regardless."

"Don't worry, I'm sure it's amazing." I would never do anything to hurt Brontë's feelings. I adore her only slightly less than Rand.

"Anything exciting happen on your trip?"

Is he fishing? My stomach is starting to churn again. I set the rest of the bottle of beer on the coffee table.

"Not really. We managed to survive the wilderness," I hedge. He studies me for a minute. I swear I'm starting to sweat from the scrutiny. How am I going to keep something this big from him? Surely he'll go back to Dansboro Crossing soon so I can have some peace.

"Okay," he says, like he doesn't believe me. "Well, I'm supposed to meet Brontë for lunch. Want to come?"

"Nah, I'm going to hang here for a little while. I'll see you at the office later."

"That works," he says, rising from the couch. "Don't forget we're taking you and Geneva to dinner later. We want to celebrate our first day as a legitimate business."

"Wouldn't miss it." Fuck, I need to miss it. I can't sit for an hour without cracking.

"Great. I'll see myself out. I'm glad you're here, buddy."

"Me too." He slaps me on the shoulder before letting himself out.

"Fuck me," I moan.

I watch the sun for another hour before heaving my ass off the couch. There's no way I'd show up at the office in sweatpants. I slide on fresh slacks from a wardrobe box. With a pressed button-down shirt, I at least look like a professional.

My facial hair is almost completely grown back out. I'll think about it later. I doubt there are any clients in the office already, but you never know. I should pass for today.

The office is empty when I arrive. I assume Geneva is still unpacking and the other two haven't made it back from lunch. Bernadette, Rand's secretary, isn't even behind her desk. That's good. It gives me a chance to wander around without being watched.

My office is the largest in the suite. It has to have room for my drafting table and computer system. I draft using both, depending on my mood. The back wall is painted blue with a cream design on it. It's perfect. Blue is one of the colors I see best. Geneva said she wanted me to be surprised, and I am.

"What do you think?" she asks from my office door.

"I think you've outdone yourself," I answer. Moving behind the computers, I try out my new desk chair. I have a drafting chair and two side chairs also.

"It's magnetic. You can put up your drawings if you need to."

"Seriously? That's genius." I spin around to try out one of the magnets from inside my desk.

"Where did you go? I came back out of the bedroom and you were gone," she says.

"I thought you were tired of me," I answer, swinging back around to face her. "I assumed you were ready for me to leave."

She stalks toward me. She's wearing a sweater dress that hits just above her knees. Black tights peek out from underneath. The fuzzy boots I love have made another appearance. When she reaches my chair, she rakes the bottom of her dress up her thighs. She places a knee on either side of my hips and straddles my lap.

"I'll never get tired of you," she purrs. "And a boyfriend should always say goodbye before he leaves." She places a kiss on the edge of my mouth.

"I'll remember that next time."

"See that you do, or when I get you home, I'll be forced to punish you." This time, she slides her tongue into my mouth when she leans back in for another kiss. My hands grab her ass, pulling her toward my aching cock. How does she get me so worked up so fast? "I'll enjoy it," she hisses.

"What in the hell?"

We both jump up from the chair hard enough that it bangs against the wall. Geneva smooths down her dress. I'm a lost cause. It's not like you can just smooth down an erection.

"Rand," I squeak. "This is not—" I don't know how to finish. This is exactly what it looks like. We couldn't even keep a secret for the day. I clear my throat and try again. "Listen, I know I made a promise. But it just happened." I'm stumbling over my words, and he's standing in the doorway with a look of rage on his face. "I can't do this, Geneva. It's giving me an ulcer."

"Fine," she snipes. She doesn't even seem the least bit rattled. "If you must know, I was thinking of fucking Peter. Again. So get over it."

"Shit, Geneva," I sputter. "Maybe a little less aggressive."

"You fucking asshole," Rand sneers. "Brontë!"

"What? I was on a phone call, Rand." She stops in the doorway to take in the drama.

"My best friend has been shagging my sister," he spits out. "When did this start?"

"Santa Fe," Geneva spits back. "Not that it's any of your business."

"Damn it, you couldn't keep it in your pants just a little while longer." I watch in shock as he pulls out his wallet. He counts out one-hundred-dollar bills. Brontë snatches them out of his hand.

"Nice doing business with you," she says to her husband. "I told you they'd never make it. Now, I've got a prospect for you on hold."

"I'm coming." He turns to face me. "Dinner's on you tonight."

"Wait." I stop him before he can leave. "Why are you not punching me in the face like you promised to do?"

"I still might, but I also see life a little differently now. There's nothing I want more than for my sister and my best friend to be happy. If they have to find that in each other, so be it. We can talk about it later, but we need the business that phone call promises. This will have to wait." He walks out of the room, leaving us in a state of confusion.

"What the hell was that?" Geneva asks.

"I have no idea."

twenty-two

GENEVA

"TO US FOR having the balls to forge our own path in life," Rand says, raising his glass of champagne. We clink glasses and take a sip. I'm not really a champagne person, but tonight feels like there's a lot to celebrate.

I can't believe how chill my brother's being about Peter and me. He even told Peter he was kidding when he told him he had to pick up the tab.

"I guess I don't understand what you've done with my brother," I say, only half in jest.

He sighs, then shakes his head. I look at Peter, sitting between us. He looks as worried as I feel. Will he break up with me if Rand demands it? He says he won't, but how do I really know?

"I'm going to warn you," Peter says. "There's nothing you can say that changes how I feel about Geneva. I under-stand why you made me swear to stay away from her. But I'm not the same man I was then."

I slide my hand into his under the table, and he squeezes it. We wait to see what Rand will say. It won't change how we feel about each other, but I don't want it to ruin a friendship either.

"Here's the deal," Rand begins. "I'm not the same man I was then either. The best thing I've ever done was follow what my heart was telling me." Brontë leans over to kiss him on the cheek. I agree, it was the best thing he's ever done.

"I've watched you circling each other for a long time. Maybe even before you realized it yourselves. At the time, all I could see was how badly it could turn out for us if you got together and then broke up. It wasn't until I fell in love that I could step back and consider what would happen if you did fall in love.

"Geneva, all I've ever wanted was for you to be safe and happy. The only man other than me I've ever trusted you with was Peter. Even knowing he wanted you, I knew he'd never hurt you. He'll never let anything bad happen to you." His brows draw together as he cocks his head at us. "Although after hearing your road trip stories, I'm starting to wonder."

"None of it was Peter's fault," I say.

"I know that, I'm just teasing you. What I'm trying to say is, who am I to stand in the way of your happiness? If you find it with the best man I've ever known, then I guess we all win."

"I appreciate that, brother," Peter says.

"Make no mistake though," Rand adds. "You do anything to hurt her, and I will set your balls on fire."

"Fair enough."

"And with that, we're going to head home so the

babysitter can do the same." Brontë stands and pulls Rand to his feet. Peter and I stand to say goodbye.

"Stay as long as you like," Rand adds. "The bill has been left open, so have dessert."

"We're so glad y'all are here," Brontë says, pulling Peter into a hug first and then me. "I can't wait for us to have some time to get to know each other even better." She turns me loose to take Rand's hand. With a wave, they leave the restaurant.

"Well," Peter says, sitting down. "Do you want to share a dessert?"

"On Rand's dime? Absolutely."

He flags down the waiter and orders a large slice of carrot cake. It arrives moments later with two coffees. I don't know if he even likes my cake of choice. It's a small thing to think of me first. It's another check on the perfect boyfriend list that's been forming in my head.

"What are your plans tomorrow at work?" he asks.

"Just get everything organized. Bernadette, of course, has done a marvelous job so far. But we're going to need a new accountant. I need to decide what HR I can handle and what should be sent out. The new logo design should be back from the graphic artist by now. I need to rattle his chain. We need business cards, letterhead, and things like that with our branding. Rand is talking about an all-new prospectus package. What?"

He's just smiling at me. He hasn't touched the other fork, which tells me the cake was for me. I haven't even seen him take a sip of his coffee. I have his full attention.

"Nothing. I'm just listening. You have so many great ideas." I blush. Wait, I'm not a blusher. Damn it. His smile grows broader.

"That works two ways," I say before this blush thing gets out of hand. "Tell me what you have planned."

"I'm supposed to work up some preliminary plans for a refit on a property in Kansas City. Rand wants to present it next week. If he lands this development, we'll fly up there to meet at the site soon."

"Who's we?"

"Brontë and I, for sure. I assume Rand."

I tamp down the niggling of jealousy that tries to make its way through my body.

"Do you have a problem with Brontë and I traveling together?" he asks.

Do I? It's obvious by the way she looks at my brother that she only has eyes for him. Besides, we're technically sisters now. She knows I won't put up with any bullshit.

"No," I say finally. "Jealousy takes too much energy."

"Good. Because I'd never cheat on you. I don't care who it's with. I only want you."

"I know." I do too. It's not just a feeling. I know that Peter could never hurt me deep in my soul. He's just not wired that way. "What say we take the rest of this cake back to your place?"

"That sounds like a great idea."

He calls for the waiter to close out the bill. Picking up the cake box, he takes my hand. I watch other women glance our way as he leads me through the restaurant. The look on their faces tells me they can sense when another catch is pulled off the market, and they're right. This catch belongs to me now.

We decide in the parking lot that I'll follow him to his new apartment. It gives me at least fifteen minutes to settle my nerves. I don't know why I'm nervous to spend the evening with Peter. It's something we've done a million times.

Maybe it's because I consider today the first official day of us. It's easy to be together when you're on vacation with one room to share. It's a whole other world to do it during ordinary day-to-day life.

We stop at a gate while he punches in a code. I follow closely through the gate behind him. Pulling into the spot next to his, I take a look at the building he now calls home. It's one of the ones I didn't get a chance to see when we were hunting for housing. It was all such a whirlwind that I barely remembered the apartment I chose.

"What do you think so far?" he asks, opening my door.

"Impressive." He ushers me into an elevator that whisks us to the top floor. The first thing I notice are the bay windows with a view of the river. His apartment definitely has a better view than mine.

"What do you think?" he asks.

"I'm not sure it can rival the Grand Canyon, but it's nice."

"One of the slips in the marina down there is mine also for when we want to go boat shopping." I smile to myself. Every time he says we, my heart thumps a little harder. "If you look to the left, you can see the south edge of downtown."

"I like it."

"Do you really?" he asks. I turn to find him watching me. "You'll be comfortable here?"

"Of course, it looks perfect to spend a lazy Sunday in," I answer. "I do have one question though."

"What's that?"

"Since we're officially a 'couple,' can we dispense with all the chit-chat until after you make me come?" His mouth opens like he wants to ask another question but then closes again before he does. I watch as his gaze turns stormy with lust. My eyes sweep down. Yep, his barometer is registering extreme interest.

Without a word, he pulls his phone from his pocket. He pushes a button and tosses it on the coffee table. He's on me before the lights finish dimming.

I'm spun around, my hands are slapped against the glass above my head, and he presses my body against it with his. He runs his hands up my body, taking my dress over my head.

"Where did these boots come from?" he growls.

"I took them to change into at the office for this very reason." They have a five-inch heel, making me the perfect height for Peter. "Did you not notice them at dinner?"

"Oh, I noticed them. Ate the whole fucking meal with a hard-on."

"Poor baby," I purr. My snark is met with a stinging slap to my right buttock. I jump against the glass. He unhooks the clasp of my bra before pushing me back against the window. My nipples pebble from the cold.

"I bet you look sexy as fuck from the water," he says. "Do you think there's some sad perv with his binoculars just waiting to see how you fuck?"

I moan; there's nothing I can do to stop it. I also can't stop how my body begins to ache for his touch. Wetness rolls down my thighs as he nips my shoulder. He kisses down my back until he's kneeling behind me.

"Let the bastard see how you come on my tongue." Then he's spreading my feet apart. He licks the moisture off my thigh with a hum.

"Peter," I beg. My clit throbs for his masterful tongue.

He rewards me with a sweep through my folds. I rock

back against him. There's another sharp sting to my backside. Then he's holding me in place as he fucks me with his tongue.

"Peter," I warn as my body begins to buzz with anticipation. He ignores it.

A tidal wave forms in my core. It races at me as he swirls, sucks, and flicks around my clit. A string of curse words rip from my mouth as the wave swallows me up. My body tumbles with the tide; light and sound are no longer accessible. Right when I think I'll drown, he's standing behind me, holding me against him.

"Better than any dessert," he hisses. "I could swallow you down for days and never get enough." He places my hands back against the window. I don't remember moving them. Then he kicks my legs back open. I don't remember stepping my legs together either.

He presses inside me. It's in my nature to fight the intrusion, but I can't. He owns me, body and soul. I turn over everything I am to his whims.

His hips crush me against the glass over and over. I can't catch my breath as I feel the waves racing toward shore again. Our bodies are slick with sweat, our hearts race together, and I never want it to end. I want Peter to take my heart as his. To keep it safe until our story is over and we find each other again in the next life.

"Give him a show, little bird. Scream for me. Shatter these windows." He reaches between my legs to pinch my clit. I do exactly as he commands. A scream rips from my lips as I shatter around him.

"Geneva," he moans. It's the last thing I hear before I'm swept away by sensations no one but he can give me.

"Geneva?" My name on his lips is also the first thing I hear. He has me cradled on his lap. We're on his couch, which is a few feet away from the bay window. I don't remember getting here. "Are you alright, sweetheart? Did I break you?"

"You did. I'm now broken for all other men," I answer. "I hope you're good with the consequences of your actions."

"I'll have to live with it, I guess." His smile is beautiful. The cerulean eyes that gaze back at me are filled with happiness. It looks amazing on him. "I didn't know you have an exhibition kink."

"Neither did I," I admit. "Good thing you're not on the first floor."

"Yeah, I talk a good game, but I don't want a bunch of strangers watching us."

"Just your dead grandma, right?" I tease.

"Exactly." He sits me on the couch and stands. "Wait here." He returns a few minutes later in a pair of sweatpants, carrying water and a long T-shirt. There's also one of his fuzzy blankets I've fallen asleep under too many times to count. "Found this in a box in the bedroom." He pulls me to him once I have the T-shirt on and tucks me under the blanket.

"Can I ask you something?" I ask as we settle in.

"Anything."

"Is this how you envisioned us being together?"

"Part of it. As much as I want to barricade us inside, we'll have to leave eventually to interact with the general public. We'll need to go on the occasional date night too. But I think we established our couple routine years ago. We just didn't realize we were a couple," he says.

"Hmm," I hum. "In that case, I think this 'us' thing is going to work out pretty satisfactory."

"Couldn't agree more." He pulls me tighter to him. "I'm glad sex is a part of it now though."

"Well, that goes without saying." We grin at each other. Then I'm pulled off the couch and tossed over his shoulder. He carries me to his bedroom and tosses me on the bed. He's on me before I'm done laughing.

Yeah, I think this relationship thing is going to work out just fine.

ONE YEAR LATER

GENEVA

I SIT in Peter's apartment, staring out the window as the sun starts to set over Lake Austin. Calling it Peter's apartment is a bit of a formality since I spend as much time here as he does. In my defense, the view is much better than from my apartment. He also has a king-size bed.

Brontë sits at the other end of the couch while Keats bounces between us. He's two now, so this is as calm as he ever gets. The kid even moves in his sleep.

"You know what?" I say, and Brontë turns to look at me. The men are at the kitchen bar, trying to pretend it's possible to hold a conversation without a toddler busting in every few seconds. "I just realized that it's an anniversary for Peter and I. Hey," I say toward the bar. "Did you know it's our anniversary?"

"Which one?" he asks. "You keep expecting me to keep

186

up with like four. First kiss, first adult kiss, the list goes on," he complains to Rand.

"Our official first normal couple day anniversary," I answer. You'd think he could at least remember that one. "As opposed to our first non-official couple anniversary." Okay, I'm starting to see what he means.

"Now, now, if y'all would just get married, you'd just have to remember one," Brontë points out.

"I figured Geneva would let me know when she's ready to get married," Peter replies.

"I'm supposed to tell you when we should get married?" I swear, I love him to the end of the earth and back, but sometimes he can be such a typical man. "Why am I responsible for that decision?"

"What would you do if I had proposed on some jumbotron six months ago?"

"I would have said no and dumped my beer on your head."

"And if I put your ring in a piece of cake and asked you while I was down on one knee in a fancy restaurant?"

"I'd probably choke on the ring and pour champagne over your head."

"Why does this always end with pouring a drink over his head?" Rand asks.

"It's better than having the ring extracted from my lower intestine after I swallow it in a piece of cake."

"Point taken."

"You know I don't like stupid public displays anyway," I continue.

"Exactly," Peter says. "So I figured when you're ready, you'll tell me how you want proposed to."

"Huh," I huff. My gaze settles back on the display over the river. Peter knows me so well. I don't remember us even discussing marriage. Do I want to get married? We have such a good thing going right now. Do I want to take a chance on messing it up? But if we're great together now, how would a piece of paper change that?

"Wait, I have a question." Brontë turns to look over the back of the couch at Peter. "If you're waiting for Geneva to tell you when to propose, how will you have a ring ready in time?"

"I have a ring already," he says.

"Really?" I ask.

"Yeah, I bought it about six months ago."

"Where is it?"

How does this make any sense? So Peter has thought enough about marrying me that he's bought a ring but has never brought the subject up? He's usually not this complicated. But then I am, and he knows that.

"In the safe in the bedroom closet." I sit glaring at him until he rolls his eyes. "I'll go get it." He disappears into the bedroom. My heart amps up to double-time when he steps back into the room with a box. "I had it made for you, but if you don't like it, we can hunt for something else." He hands me the box.

Slowly, I open the lid. Brontë gasps, but I can't even get enough oxygen in my lungs for that. It's not the typical gold and diamond engagement ring.

I slip it on my finger so I can study it better. It's white gold that looks silver. In the center is a large onyx stone with two smaller diamonds on either side of it. Accent diamonds swirl around them, encasing the main stones. It's simply the most stunning ring I've ever seen.

"It couldn't be like anyone else's," he says. "You're not like anyone else. It has to be as unique as you are."

I swallow back tears as I stare at it. Brontë picks up

Keats and moves to the bar next to Rand. It's just Peter and I in the living room now.

"I don't want to take it off," I whisper.

"Then this is you telling me it's time." Peter takes my hand and pulls me to the bay window I've fallen in love with. He gets down on one knee, taking my hands in his. "Geneva Selene Randolph," he begins.

No, the fact that my initials stand for gunshot residue has not been lost on me.

"I knew from the first day you walked into my office in San Francisco and reamed me a new one for missing the deadline on the Holland building that I was going to spend the rest of my life with you. I just wasn't sure how to do that.

"I fell in love with you then, and that's never changed. This last year has been the best of my life. I don't want it to ever end. Will you marry me so it never will?"

Tears are rolling down my face. I'm not sure I've ever cried tears of happiness until this year. Of course, the answer is yes. But that doesn't mean I'm going to be too easy to get. After all, a girl needs to always keep her man on his toes. Peter would be disappointed if I didn't.

"Am I expected to move in here?" I ask, raising one eyebrow.

"Yes," he answers. I can see the corner of his mouth turn up slightly. He knows what I'm doing. "Fine, we can get a place big enough for your workout studio." He rolls his eyes.

"But we'll have to give up this window."

"There are bigger houses on the lake with windows." His smile spreads across his face.

"How about—"

"Geneva," I hear three voices ring out. I sink to my knees with a laugh.

"Then I'd better answer yes. I will marry you, Peter Winsloe." I press my lips to his. His arms wrap around my waist, pulling me against him. "Do we get to honeymoon at the Grand Canyon?" I ask when he releases me.

"No," he answers. "But I'm game to do some hiking in Waimea Canyon, Kauai. When I'm not too busy wrestling that Brazilian bikini off of you, that is."

"You've got a deal, Winsloe."

"Good to hear, Randolph." Then his lips are back on mine.

* * *

PETER

Most people would think I'm insane for letting Geneva decide when we get engaged. But then they don't know her like I do. She lets me tie her up in bed, but I have to give back what I take. She just as often ties me down.

Growing up with no control in life does funny things to a person. It takes a tremendous amount of trust for her to let me in, and I don't take that for granted.

It's also an odd choice to choose onyx for the main stone in an engagement ring, but Geneva is not like anyone I've ever known. I knew the ring had to speak to her on a level that says I know her heart. Anything less would never do. I also didn't want whatever drink was nearest dumped on my head for getting it wrong.

The tears still rolling down her face as she holds her hand out for Brontë speaks volumes. I knew she wouldn't want a public display, but having her brother here to share the moment was perfect. I caught him wiping away a tear or two also.

I suspect we'll have a small wedding with just family. I wonder if she'll even invite her father. It's a given that I'll have Tim and Rand by my side, of course. But I suspect she won't stand for anyone to give her away.

"So after all of these years of acting like brothers, we're finally going to become them?" Rand asks, shaking my hand. I pull him into a hug. After all, brothers hug, and this man is as close as a brother to me as my biological one. "Ooh, you'll be the baby one at that since I beat you by a couple of months."

"I still outweigh you by a good fifty pounds though. Keep that in mind." He laughs and slaps me on the back. I can probably bench press him too, but I'll let that go. "Thanks, man, for not holding me to that promise," I add.

"Pssh. I think that was the best move I made. She's all your problem now. No takebacks."

"I heard that, asshat," Geneva says from across the room.

Rand winces and ducks behind me. It's all in fun though. Their love was built through the need to survive together. It's unique and special. I would never come between them.

"We should go out to celebrate," Brontë announces. "Let me see if I can get the sitter for a few hours."

Rand moves to her side as she dials. Keats jumps from the couch into his arms.

"Think we can pull off a wedding in three months?" Geneva asks, sliding her arms around my neck.

"That fast?"

"I want to get to Hawaii before the crowds hit. It'll just be family anyway and a few friends."

"Baby, I'll marry you wherever, whenever, and with whomever you want."

"You just keep getting better with age, Winsloe." She kisses me quickly before pulling back. We did have to promise Rand no more public displays after he almost walked in on me between her thighs on my desk.

"I hope so, Randolph. It's not like I can get any younger." I know my soon-to-be sister-in-law is in the process of setting up a babysitter, but all I want to do is get my fiancée spread out on the bed. It's weird how easily that word rolls off my tongue. Fiancée. It has a nice ring to it. Wife will sound even better.

"So three months," I say. "Well, if anyone can pull off a wedding in that time, it's you."

"Damn straight," Rand adds. "My sister can do anything she sets her mind on."

"Tell me something I don't know."

Her face lights up at our words. Rand and I tell her this all the time. At first, she ignored us, but we've been wearing her down. I don't let the sun go down without reminding her every day of everything she has accomplished.

Our business is thriving, thanks to her direction. We've found a group of friends because of her ability to nurture our social circle. She's even getting the hang of slipping the word "y'all" into everyday language.

"Success!" Brontë announces. "We'll drop Keats off and meet you downtown in a few?"

"Sounds perfect," Geneva says.

"Come on." Brontë hustles Keats and Rand out the door. The lock barely clicks behind them before Geneva is pulling her shirt over her head. Grabbing my hand, she tugs me toward the bedroom.

"Clothes off, Peter. There's just enough time for that

quickie we talked about on the way through the mountains."

Be jealous. She's that amazing. I toe my shoes off before jogging to the bedroom after her. I don't bother to unbutton my shirt; I just pull it off over my head. She'll be slick already, waiting for me.

I know she'll still be up for more when we finally get home tonight. The best thing I've ever done is throw my integrity out the window on that snowy evening in Santa Fe.

I've never regretted that decision. I'd do it all again if it meant I'd still wind up with the gorgeous woman waiting on our bed on all fours. Did I think for a minute when we left San Francisco that I'd wind up here? Not for a second. Did I expect to lure Geneva into my bed? Not really. But I'm glad I'm the lucky bastard that did.

"Hurry, Peter. I need you inside me," she moans, rocking toward where I've stepped to the edge of the bed. I slide inside. It never gets old knowing I'll never get enough of her.

Finally, I'm that bastard that got the girl. A truly lucky bastard.

* * *

Thank you for reading Falling. I hope you enjoyed Peter and Geneva's story. Want more of the Dansboro Crossing series? Start at the beginning with *Overdue*, here: https://book s2read.com/u/4D8v6P

Don't miss another release. Sign up for my newsletter here: https://www.averysamson.com/contact

also by avery samson

<u>The Dansboro Crossing Series</u>

Overdue

Upshot

Brazen

Harmony for Christmas

<u>The New England Romance Series</u>

Nothing Ventured

Best Laid Schemes

In For a Penny

Actions Speak Louder

<u>The Sideswiped Series</u>

Hers to Take

Hers to Keep

Hers to Win

Hers to Tame

Hers to Crave

Hers to Forget

Writing as A. Samson

<u>The Inhuman Protectors Romance Series</u>

Intangible

Invincible

Combustible

Justifiable

<u>The Sköll Ranch Shifter Series</u>

Sten

Dane

Arne

acknowledgments

I bet you finished Peter and Geneva's story wondering where the small town in this small-town romance is. Technically, it's in *Upshot* where you're introduced to Rand's best friend and sister. I couldn't resist seeing where their flirty banter went. At the end of Upshot, they decide to begin again in Austin. So, road trip!

Every book I write I envision their readers spending a lazy afternoon curled up in another world. Thank you for choosing *Falling* to spend your day with. I love all of the reviews, emails, and in-person meets during book signings with each and every one of you.

A huge shout out to Ellie at My Brother's Editor for taking the time to polish all of the commas, reversed sentence structures, and repeating words. There's no way I could continue without her hard work.

Thanks to Jane Ashley Photography for the beautiful photo of Peter and Geneva (Carlus & Josie). It took me a lot of time to find the perfect one.

Big thank you to all of the readers, ARC readers, reviewers, bloggers, and everyone else who helps me spread the word about *Falling*. I very much appreciate the time you spend in my world.

Finally, thanks to my family for all the support, love, and time they spend talking me off that proverbial cliff. Thomas, Wilson, Madison, Conor, and especially Rachel, I couldn't do it without you. Love to you always.

Avery Samson grew up on a ranch outside of a small west Texas town. Since she could remember, she's had her face stuck in a book. High School graduation found her leaving ranch life for the big city.

After living all over the state of Texas, she now finds herself back on one of the family ranches near Dallas with her husband surrounded by cattle. A lot of them. They're everywhere! When not traveling or reading, she spends her time writing.

Avery would love for you to follow her. She's everywhere (just like those damn cows.)

Join my newsletter for all the latest news.
averysamsonbooks.com/newsletter

Visit my website for my current book list.
averysamsonbooks.com

Join my reader group.
https://www.facebook.com/groups/216191437248096

Like me on Facebook.
https://www.facebook.com/averysamsonauthor

Follow me on Instagram.
https://www.instagram.com/averysamson91/

Watch my videos on TikTok.
https://www.tiktok.com/@averysamson91

Check out my Pinterest page.
https://www.pinterest.com/averysamson91/

www.ingramcontent.com/pod-product-compliance
Lightning Source LLC
Chambersburg PA
CBHW031600310726
48974CB00003B/756